The White Tiger Chronicles
Book Two

WRATH OF THE WHITE TIGER

Nigel Hywel-Jones

Published by Big Wall Publishing

Wrath of the White Tiger

Edited by

Iain Donnelly @ Saraswati Publishing

Siem Reap, Cambodia

Cover Art by Rebecca Coughlan @ WorthwHyle Marketing

ACKNOWLEDGEMENTS

Wrath of the White Tiger concludes this particular episode in Charli's life. Again, there are many who read this story and encouraged me over the years. However, as this story concludes I must single out Ira and Judy Denton – a brain surgeon and a rocket scientist. Ira and Judy were first introduced to the World of Charli about fifteen years ago.

But from 2013 to 2016, they worked with me to fine tune Charli's story to almost what it is today. What is presented to you, the reader, is thanks to Ira and Judy but also thanks to my editor Iain Donnelly, who worked so closely with me to finally bring this across the line.

This conclusion to the story still has a secret dedication to an inspiration. Maybe one day in the future, I will reveal that inspiration. For now, I leave matters to…

The Ghost of the White Tiger.

WRATH OF THE WHITE TIGER

Prologue

On a flight from Thailand to London, a young Thai girl (Lek) falls ill as the plane is landing. After a doctor helps and they land, it's discovered that the girl has heroin-filled condoms inside her. The doctor (Sir John Cormack) is passed a note that the girl gave to an airhostess with details of a London contact. The paper results in John Cormack becoming involved with (Charlotte) Charli Harris.

Four months later, Charli and Cormack return Lek's ashes to Thailand. It was her dying wish that her ashes should be returned to her native soil. Cormack has had a close association with Thailand for over 30 years, while Charli has been visiting for four years.

Charli takes Cormack to Chaiyaphum Province and they meet Lek's father who is now the only inhabitant of an abandoned village that used to nestle in a small, forested valley.

Lek's simple life was turned upside down when businessmen cleared the surrounding forest. For a short time, the village enjoyed prosperity, but corruption destroyed it and its inhabitants drifted away as the logging was completed, leaving a dust-bowl valley with only Lek and her father living in it.

Charli and Cormack take a trip across the valley and up the hill to a waterfall where Lek used to hide from her problems. As she leaves, she looks over her shoulder and sees a vision that Lek gave her – a Ghost Memory. Alive and green with a six-year-old Lek and an old white tiger that Lek had told her of coming across. Before returning to Bangkok, Charli is confronted by a super-confident Lek and a White Tiger in a Ghost Dream. After this she is obligated to help Lek's father and to help Lek's memories.

In Bangkok, Cormack introduces Charli to the family with whom he has long been associated. Her initial meeting is with the daughter (Jay), who inhabits a different world to that of Lek. Her father (Yai) has connections with the government and military while her Grandmother Djim is the matriarch of this very small family.

Charli recounts to Jay how she first came to Thailand at the time of the suicide of Sir Gordon Wessel of Wessel Enterprises. This was also the first time she met Steven Hunt. Hunt was presented with Lek after his business dealings. Hunt, however, after seeing Charli, passed Lek to a colleague. From then, he tries many ways to get to Charli. A favourite sobriquet of his for her is the Ice Maiden.

Charli continues to resist Hunt's attempts at seducing her and it becomes apparent there is far more to this smooth-talking Lothario than meets the eye. A tangled web is beginning to weave its way from the UK to Thailand and it isn't yet clear who sits at the centre awaiting unsuspecting prey.

Chapter 1

Jay looked at Charli in shock. Hers was a privileged world; she lived in a cocoon of wealth and entitlement. Violence was something she only witnessed at a distance from the disassociated comfort of a taxi home from one of the city's elite nightclubs. The violence and transactional sex of Bangkok were as alien to Jay as Thailand had been to Charli on her first visit.

Jay knew the sex trade existed but she had always assumed it was just paying money for sex, no more, no less. The idea that men existed who would take pleasure in inflicting such violence on someone they obviously saw as little more than a piece of meat to do with as they will had shocked her to her core.

"God. Charli. I'm sorry I didn't know. You must think I'm a real arsehole. I've never met a bar girl. This Steven guy sounds like a real shit."

"I'm not sure about that, Jay. He's just a self-absorbed prick if you ask me. But the real shit was that fucking bastard that he passed Lek over to."

"You bet."

They ordered more drinks. The questions continued from Jay. And the more she interrogated Charli, the more Charli realised this girl from her privileged family knew little of the lives of her fellow Thai. As with so many of the Bangkok upper classes, she regarded the lower classes from the despised Northeast as barely essential nuisances. Good only for maids, taxi drivers, and construction workers. These people, these ants, cluttered up Bangkok. They made Bangkok dirty with their noodle stalls on the streets. Charli was opening her eyes to a whole new world and Charli hoped that Jay's new comprehension may elicit some empathy and understanding.

The over-confident Jay had spent almost half of her life in another country getting an education that was itself highly privileged and beyond the means of most ordinary Britons. It was little wonder she had no idea of Lek's life.

The more that Jay questioned Charli the more Charli knew the direction that the evening was going to take.

And so it was that at ten in the evening, the taxi dropped them at the end of a street that has given the whole of Bangkok, if not the whole of Thailand, its reputation; Patpong. At first, Charli had been reluctant to take Jay. But Jay had insisted and Charli decided it was time she was educated. They walked down the crowded street filled with market stalls, tourists, and stunningly dressed Thai women. Charli threaded her way through the crowd and Jay followed. Red, pink, blue, white, and yellow neon flashed everywhere. Each place advertising 'pussy' or 'foxy' or 'sexy'. 'Lady', 'Girl', 'Love'. The same group of words in different but ever-sleazy combinations.

A tout squeezed his way over to Charli. He held a card in front of her face. "You see sex show, lady? Number one sexy show in Thailand. I take you see."

Charli shook her head at him. She tried to carry on, pushing her way through the crowd of men and women. Old and young. Fat and thin. Farang and Thai. Jay held back, watching the scene unfold.

"You no pay, lady. My bar no have cover charge. You look. Fuck-show number one. You no like, no stay, okay?

Charli carried on, trying to make her way through the crowd. She noted that Jay kept her small shoulder purse close to her, distrustful of thieves. The tout was insistent. Charli turned to him. She smiled. She took the card from his hand and studied it. She already knew what was written on it.

'Pussy drink bottle'

'Pussy open bottle'

'Pussy use chopstick'

'Pussy writing'

'Pussy smoking'

'Pussy play trumpet'

'Pussy shot balloon'.

The list went on...

"You've some well-trained felines in your bar."

The joke was completely lost on him.

"Number one in Thailand, I promise no bullshit, lady."

Charli gave him the card back and grimaced.

"This very naughty. I should not see. Not good. Me nice lady, same-same also my friend. Okay?"

"Yes good. Manchester United number one for England. America number one for the world. My bar number one for Thailand. I no bullshit you. I show you. Show friend also."

He turned to Jay and spoke to her in Thai. Jay stared dumbly at him and then replied in English.

"Sorry, I no speakee Thai. I Filipina."

Jay was absorbed and having fun. Charli continued to push her way through the crowd. She knew exactly where she was going to take Jay and she would not be taken to any other bar by a tout. Most of the touts took unsuspecting customers to places which then extorted them with a large bill at the end. A large bill for the show and an inflated bill for the drinks. No different to Soho in London.

"I don't want fuck-show okay. I take my friend some place. Okay? No want fuck-show. So, fuck off. Okay?"

Jay held her hand over her mouth, trying to stifle a laugh. Charli had heard the stories of people getting scalped. There were many upstairs clubs that had seedy sex shows. But Charli knew the bar that Lek had worked at. She also knew a few others that Lek had told her were safe to go to. There were some 'reputable' upstairs bars where the customer paid only for the drinks and were not conned at the end of the evening.

And it was to one of these that Charli was now headed. She reached a set of wooden steps. She looked up at the sign just to make sure it was the same one. That it had not been taken over or sold out and changed its name. Something that often happened in such an unstable business environment.

'Galactic Pussy'.

Charli turned to Jay.

"Are you ready Jay? We're here."

She walked up the darkened stairs and Jay followed. The tout, who had continued to follow them, looked on in stunned amazement.

"You crazy fucking lesbian, dyke, bitch, et cetera, et cetera. Fuck me. You say you no want fucky-show. This my fucking bar I want fucking take you. You one crazy fucking Farang lady."

He continued to himself in Thai. Jay laughed. She understood what he was saying, and it was not flattering to either of them. At the top of the stairs, a petite girl sat with a blue artificial silk wraparound. She smiled sadly at Charli as she pushed open the door but glared contemptibly at Jay. Jay looked over her shoulder at the girl as she went in. She had rarely come across such poorly-concealed hatred. She felt goosebumps and, for a moment, wanted to turn and leave. She, however, trusted Charli not to take her anywhere dangerous.

Inside was black. And cold. The walls were harsh with ultraviolet lighting. The room smelled of stale beer and staler sweat. For Jay, who had lived in a single-sex school, it also brought back the smell of women who lived their lives together. It was a very brief sensation that passed, frighteningly, through her body. She shuddered.

Mirrors covered the walls and the ceiling, making the small room look larger. A bench seat and small tables surrounded the wall. In the middle was a single stage with a bar around it. Charli indicated that they should sit at the bar. On the central stage were six girls. Their dancing was uninspired. They were bored and merely going through the motions.

One, a fatter one, had more animation than the others. She danced with some eroticism up against one of the two silvered poles at either end of the stage. The girls were dressed in a variety of clothing. One was fully clothed in a pale blue swimsuit. A short dumpy girl wore white knickers but was topless. Her tiny breasts stuck out in front of her. There was a vacant look in her face as she stared intently at her reflection in the wall mirror. Another with very long sleek hair that fell to the small of her back danced in a sequinned G-string. No top. Jay admired her figure. The best of the lot. She had long legs made even longer because of the G-string. A small waist and breasts that were not too small or too big. Jay watched her approvingly. But the girl moved with the same bored detachment of the others. Only the fat one dressed fully in the blue swimsuit moved with conviction.

Charli ordered two beers. Jay followed her example of drinking from the bottle, but only after carefully wiping the rim with a tissue. Jay watched everything with fascination. Charli had seen it all before. There was, for her, no need, or real desire, to watch so closely. She did not want to stay for too long here. Only long enough for Jay to see what she had come to watch. The 'pussy' shows. While Jay watched in fascination, Charli's mind could not help but wander back to thoughts of Lek and her short sad life lived out of this same bar.

When they left 30 minutes and a beer each later, Charli was glad that it had not progressed into an extended stay. It easily could have done because it was obvious that Jay was infected by the place. She questioned Charli about the downstairs bars. These did not have sex shows. Only Go-Go dancers. They had a drink in one place. For Jay.

Although there was no sex, there were plenty of bodies. And Jay noted that in these downstairs bars the girls were, generally, more beautiful than those upstairs. They moved with far more sensuality. They probably cost a lot more. They ended the evening at an outside bar, where they could watch the night go by. The bar they chose seemed to be popular with Katoey – Lady Boys. Jay pointed these out to Charli as if Charli had no idea of the Katoey of Bangkok.

As they sat at the bar, two men sat next to them. Both had shaved heads and their bare arms were tattooed. The elder one had a nose that had obviously been broken several times in fights. His friend, trying to appear confident, looked out of place. They ordered two beers. Grinning stupidly, the younger one took a swig from his bottle and almost fell off his stool as he turned to his friend to speak.

"Fuckin' hell, Mike, this is some fuckin' place. I'll tell you, some fuckin' place. I never dreamed that I'd see so much pussy in one fuckin' place. And what's more, they're all up for it. Thanks, Mike, you're a real pal, a real fuckin' mate, I won't…"

He stopped briefly to hold his breath and stifle a hiccough.

"…. ever fuckin' forget this."

He raised his beer to his friend.

"S'all right, Kev. No problem. Yer first fuckin' time at sea. First decent fuckin' port of call is fuckin' Bangkok. Yer twentieth fuckin' birthday last week too. What could I fuckin' do? Bring you here. That's what. Fuckin' shit, get a load of what's comin' over your way."

A stunning body moved in on the two men. She sat next to 'Kev'. Her movements had a highly exaggerated sexiness that would have given Mae West a strong challenge at any time of her life from eighteen to eighty. The Thai oozed sensuality from every opening. She held out her hand. It hung delicately in front of the two sailors waiting to be taken. She smiled. A pure white flash of polished teeth.

"Hi. My name Julie. You name?"

Kev gagged into his bottle of beer. He had never been so close to anything as beautiful as this before. He remembered having fallen in love with the cartoon character of Jessica Rabbit when he was a teenager. He had the same sensation now. Maybe it was because of the manner in which Julie moved; like Mae West and like Jessica Rabbit. How she smelled and the way she moved made his pants go tight. He had never dared to admit to Mike but he was still a virgin. Kev quietly told himself that this was going to be the night when he would finally lose it.

He slid his head into his right arm and looked at Mike.

"Fuckin' hell Mike. Help mate. What do I fuckin' do?"

Mike grinned at him. He raised his bottle in congratulations. He smiled.

"It's up to you, mate. I think you've scored there. Offer her a fuckin' drink. That's what I'd fuckin' do. You fuckin' lucky fuckin' barsteward. First time in fuckin' Bangkok and you fuckin' score. You fuckin' lucky fuckin' bar-steward. That's what you are mate."

Charli could hear this exchange. She smiled into her drink and turned to look at Jay. Jay was still surprised at the whole evening; her eyes were elsewhere taking in the whole sordid street scene. Jay tried to look along the bar at the development without making herself so obvious. Charli grinned at Jay. She grinned back at Charli.

Kev turned back to the woman.

He took her hand and planted a polite kiss on the back of it. He felt embarrassed. Despite knowing what he wanted to do with the woman, he was still very shy at the whole thought of how to break the ice and especially of what was to come.

He belched.

"Sorry. Hi."

He smiled at her.

She nodded at him. She withdrew her hand.

"Hi. I Julie. You name?"

"Kevin. Kev."

He smiled at her again, tried to wink, and steadied himself on the swivel stool. He stared openly, obviously, at her body. Packed tightly into a black backless PVC mini dress. The sides were open making him realise that, apart from her shoes, this was the only item of clothing she was wearing. No bra, no knickers, just the mini dress and a pair of shoes. His trousers tightened some more.

"Kevin-Kev? Me thirsty. You buy me beer?"

He grinned stupidly at her and turned to Mike for encouragement. Mike stuck a thumb up and grinned. Kevin turned back to the woman.

"Sure. No problem."

The woman swivelled the seat to face him and sat with her legs slightly apart. He looked at the tight PVC that was stretched across her thighs as she rocked the swivel to the left and right. She placed her hand on his thigh and delicately moved her fingers up. She smiled at him as she gripped his crotch and massaged him. He smiled inanely and shuddered uncomfortably.

Mike had turned back to face the bar. The gooseberry for the night. He stared at his bottle and grinned to himself. He watched as the woman continued to massage his friend's crotch. After a short while, he looked around. His eye caught Charli's. She raised her bottle in salute.

"Hi, Mike."

Mike looked sheepishly at her. Embarrassed. He was uncomfortable talking with women. Working on ships for almost seven years since leaving school, he had never had a female friend. He never knew what to say to women as he spent most of his time trying to consider the cheapest way to get them into bed with him. For this reason, most of his conquests had been prostitutes.

He briefly noted Charli. He thought to himself that his chances with her would be zero. There was a certain class of woman with whom he could never expect to score. Beauty at a distance, unreachable and unattainable. She was part of that class. Educated, moneyed, and suspicious of all men. He could not even recall having had a conversation with one before. And now she was speaking to him.

Charli considered carefully what to say next. She looked at his broken nose and the scar on his neck. This was a man who had seen some fights before, and what she was about to say could be an invitation for a fight.

"Do you know what you've hooked your friend up with there? A Katoey. You know what one of those is?"

A grin stretched from ear to ear. Mike had had some beer to drink. But he was in a better state than his younger friend, who was now being gently mauled by the 'girl'. He looked straight at Charli.

"Yep. I know."

He whispered.

"I... I've been to Bangkok many times before. This is Kevin's first visit. I know all about Katoeys. Ladyboys. Boys that have had their dicks chopped off. Ssshhh."

He held a finger to his lips and winked at Charli. He grinned stupidly at her. Charli grinned back. She raised her almost empty bottle to him.

"You know, Mike? You're a real fucking bastard. You really are. Aren't you?"

Charli smiled at him as she said this. She knew that if anybody else, male or female, had called him a 'real fucking bastard' they would most likely have woken up in hospital. But Charli was confident in her ability to control the situation. He grinned and nodded to her.

"Yep. I am. He'll get a fuckin' shock when he fuckin' finds out. An even bigger fuckin' shock if he fuckin' wakes up with her. With him. With it. Whatever."

Jay had been paying attention to what was being said. Their drinks almost finished, Charli paid. As they left, young Kevin was enjoying his first sexual experience with a person other than himself.

Less than 24 hours later, he was nursing a lot of bruises after trying to pick a fight with his mate Mike and was churning over in his mind whether he should go for an HIV test.

Chapter 2

Following Jay's education in Patpong, Charli noted that when they now went out together, she dressed more and more outrageously. Although Jay was 22, she acted more like a 14-year-old. Charli was surprised at such immaturity. Surprised, especially when she compared Jay's behaviour with that of Lek who had been mature beyond her younger years.

It took Jay time to find a backless and sideless PVC dress such as the one the Katoey had worn. But she was resourceful and when she found the dress, she delighted in challenging a number of Bangkok's finer restaurants with it.

The first time that Jay wore her 'new favourite dress' was when she arranged to meet Charli at the Peking Royal Hotel before going on to its downstairs discotheque. It was a popular haunt for the young rich of Bangkok who had to be seen. Charli arrived late and was shocked to see Jay wearing the dress in the lobby of what was one of Bangkok's classier Chinese hotels. She sat down opposite Jay. Jay called one of the waitresses over with an imperious wave.

"I want one beer Singha for my friend. Another Hennessy for me."

The waitress spoke to Jay in Thai. Jay glared at her.

"You speak to me in English, okay? I know you can speak to me rudely in Thai. But you have to be polite in English. So, speak English. Khao jai ka?"

As the waitress walked away, Charli glared at Jay disapprovingly. Jay looked back at her.

"Charli. My country is so fucking obsessed with appearance. With being polite. With being normal and not challenging the system. You know? That stuck-up fucking bitch has been treating me like a bar girl all bloody evening."

Charli interrupted her.

"What do you expect? I'm sorry Jay. But you have to admit, it's a bit over the top. It is a bit on the Patpong Bar Girl side."

"Charli, that's not the bloody point. The point is, father could buy this bloody hotel. The point is, I shouldn't have to apologise for the way I dress for a few bloody country-bumpkin waitresses. That, Charli, is the point. They're here to do a job. And that job is to serve me. Irrespective of the way I'm dressed."

Charli considered how irrational and, especially, how immature this argument was and decided it was best not to pursue matters. She was in no mood for an argument. She had been late because she had been tied up with Steven Hunt in the lobby of her hotel. As inappropriate as Jay's clothes were for the lobby bar of a posh Chinese hotel, they were in keeping, just, with a high society discotheque, which is what this hotel boasted in its basement.

And after Jay had made a point of embarrassing the waitress further, it was to this discotheque - The Forbidden City - that they moved on to. Charli felt sorry for the poor waitress who had only been doing her job. As the waitress lowered her eyes and gave a polite wai to Jay, which was not acknowledged, Charli slipped her a large tip, which was gratefully received. The waitress smiled at the beautiful, kind foreigner as Charli moved to catch up with the indignant Jay.

They took the lift down to the basement. To a place that tried to convince everyone that it was the number one discotheque in Bangkok. It was not. There were several number one discotheques in Bangkok and they were all basically the same. All the number ones were the same in that they were pale imitations of a truly international high society discotheque. Even Jay conceded that these places could not compete with any of the top clubs in London. Charli agreed. For a while, a few years before, she had been a regular visitor at several nightclubs frequented by London's rich, famous or infamous. Nightclubs where the Princess of Wales and the

Duchess of York could be seen relaxing because the press dare not trouble them in such places.

Inside was black. And cold. The walls were harsh with ultraviolet lighting. The room, however, did not smell of stale beer. Mirrors covered the walls and the ceiling, making the large room look even larger. Jay directed Charli to a separate room; the adjoining restaurant. This enjoyed all the atmosphere of the discotheque but without the crowd on the floor. They had a table reserved. Observing the scene, Charli could tell that Jay was a regular. She was noticed.

"Oh, hi Jay. Not seen you here for a while."

Charli had to look twice. His voice sounded like Val Kilmer doing an impersonation of Jim Morrison. Laid-back, slightly drugged Los Angeles. He was tall and wore an expensive jacket in a broad-shouldered style that seemed not to fit. In one hand was a Hennessy. In the other was a mobile telephone. He was Thai but spoke English to Jay. Jay smiled at him. Out of politeness for Charli's presence, she also spoke English.

"Nikki. How are you? I've been looking after my friend, Charli. Charli? This is Nikki. An old friend. Old friend aren't you, Nikki?"

Charli nodded to him. She considered, briefly, extending her hand but decided not to give him the challenge of how to shake hands with a glass in one and his microwave emitting, brain-destroying Excalibur in the other. It was the size of a small brick and probably weighed as much.

"Yeah. Say, err... Jay? Is this a good time to bell your old man? I mean. I've these options. You know? And I…… think he might like, erm… to take a look before the rest of the crowd do. You know what I mean? Get in early. What d'you think, Jay?"

Jay's face went serious.

"Please, Nikki, another time. I want to enjoy myself. I don't want to talk about my fucking father. He saw my new dress and went ape-shit. I mean totally ape-shit, big-big time. He's threatening to cut my allowance and lower the limit on my card. Can you believe that? Twenty-two and he's threatening me because of a dress. I mean, it's not like I'm a 14-year-old schoolgirl."

Nikki laughed at this.

"Yeah, right. Okay, another time maybe. Catch you later, Jay. Oh... the dress? It's cool."

He wandered off, trying to find another friend to talk to.

Jay watched him as he went. She turned to Charli.

"Maybe the loneliest guy in the room, Charli. Spends his time drifting from 'friend' to 'friend'. Spending time on the edge of a conversation before moving on to the next. Sometimes I feel sorry for him. Other times I think; so what? He's a nothing. What was it that group, the Rolling Stones, used to sing about? Nowhere Man?"

Charli chose not to correct Jay, but watched as he stopped by another crowd of people. Everyone greeted him with a smile and the same 'please go away soon' politeness.

A few years later, when the Asian economies melted down, Nikki lost all his money in the stock-exchange crash. After his girlfriend walked out on him and after his prized Mercedes Benz had been repossessed, he took the public bus round to the Stock Exchange of Thailand, walked into the lobby, pulled out a gun and shot himself in the head. A disgrace to his family, his father disowned him and refused to have him admitted to the private hospital that he owned. He had Nikki admitted, instead, to a government hospital and forbade any member of the family to visit him. Nikki struggled with life for 11 days before dying two days short of his 27th birthday.

Jay ordered a selection of Chinese dishes for them. They nibbled at these. They talked, they drank, and they danced.

That evening at the discotheque, Jay's dress was a winner. Everyone who knew her came to see her. Or more importantly, to see the dress. They all paid polite attention to Charli. Some were uncomfortable speaking to the silent foreigner as it showed up the limitations in their English. It was Jay that they were interested in. Jay and her dress. There were a few who had cameras. And they wanted their picture taken. With Jay. With 'the dress'. And Charli could see that Jay loved every minute of the attention.

"You've many friends, Jay. I hadn't realised."

Charli spoke above the sudden burst of overly loud live music.

"Absolutely, Charli. But I think my dress has more friends. I'm not stupid. I've got eyes and can see also."

She smiled at Charli. Charli smiled back. Trying to decide whether she admired what Jay had done or whether she thought she was reckless.

Later in the evening, Jay pointed out a group of loud men who were beginning to make a nuisance of themselves. Charli was fascinated by their oafishness and stared openly in their direction. Watching, as Charli stared at them, Jay began to get worried. She spoke.

"Charli, it's not good to stare at them. They're trouble. Big trouble. Please, stop it."

Jay's warning was too late. The head of the pack had seen Charli staring and wandered, a little unsteadily, over to their table.

Unsure of himself, he stared at Charli. Jay looked across at Charli and was horrified to see that her friend continued to stare straight into the eyes of the drunken Thai. It had already turned into a contest to see who would blink first. His friends, seven of them, had now sauntered over to Jay's table and were watching the outcome.

Unsure of what to do, Jay surreptitiously arranged for the bill from a passing waitress. As the drunken Thai realised he was about to lose the staring contest, he broke eye contact with Charli, blinked, and turned to Jay, speaking to her in Thai.

"What was he asking you, Jay?"

"Please, Charli, say nothing. It's best we leave. I've got the bill already."

The drunken Thai looked on at the two of them in some confusion. It became clear to Charli that he could not speak, or understand, any English and with that realisation she felt stronger against him.

"What did Johnnie Walker say to you, Jay?"

"Charli, don't. Please. He asked me if you knew who he was."

Johnnie Walker stood, uncertainly, waiting for an answer.

Charli looked at him, smiled and then turned her attention to his friends. As she spoke English, she felt sure that at least one of the seven Neanderthals would be able to understand her and would be able to report her words to Johnnie.

"Oh yes, I do know who Johnnie Walker is. Johnnie's the son of some ex-policeman turned politician. Johnnie, his brother, and some friends were involved in a brawl in Pattaya the other year when somebody refused to pay them due respect. If I recall, it had something to do with accidentally stepping on Johnnie's foot which caused him some upset. I'm not surprised. By the look of you, Johnnie, your foot's probably where you keep what passes for your brain.

Anyhow, the poor guy ended up in hospital with several broken ribs and a smashed skull. Although he brought charges against Johnnie, he later dropped them when he realised that delayed amnesia (a first of its kind) had meant he could no longer be sure who had ordered the kicking. I'm sure that the three grenades which apparently fell into his parent's, his sister's and his girlfriend's garden had nothing to do with the delayed amnesia. I think the police put the grenades down to El Niño. Anyway, charges were dropped against Johnnie and his friends. I think it involved a gun as well, but I'm not really sure. I tend to forget those little details.

Then, five or six months ago, I do believe Johnnie managed to get his picture in the paper once more. This time a gun really was involved. That was also over some incident in a pub and involved Johnnie having the victim beaten to the ground. If I recall correctly, Johnnie then held the victim's head to the floor with his foot while he pulled a gun out and calmly shot the poor guy in the head. Again, as I remember, Johnnie managed to have the guy conveniently forget whose foot it was that stood on his head and whose finger it was that pulled the trigger that blew away most of his right lower jaw.

Now, I've already written Johnnie off as a mentally deficient sub-Neanderthal with an IQ slightly less than that of the average amoeba. But I'm sure that some of you guys, his 'friends', will have a little more grey matter and will realise that if he pulls some stunt against a foreigner, and a woman at that, he, and you, might just not get away with it so easily this fucking time. Khao jai ka? Do any of you understand?"

The bill arrived, and Jay was fumbling to pay it. Charli took the bill, folded it, and told the waitress that there had been a mistake. She wanted more drinks. The waitress, knowing who was standing in front of the table, was only too glad to run off.

"Welcome to The Land of Smiles. Now, will one of you 'Friends of Johnnie' please explain to the sub-Neanderthal that I'd like him to go back across the room and to leave me and my friend in peace?"

One of the seven moved forward and spoke quietly to Johnnie Walker. Jay heard the conversation and relaxed at what she heard. She whispered to Charli that he had told Johnnie Walker that she, Charli, had thought he was some superstar who is in a Johnnie Walker advert on television.

The man then moved forward, sat down opposite Charli and Jay and spoke briefly to Jay, telling her what he had already told Johnnie Walker. He then turned to Charli and spoke in English.

"Please, Miss, you're very brave but a little crazy to say what you did. My friend is hot-headed, and he'd not have cared whether you are a woman and, or, a Farang. He has a gun, and he'd not think twice about using it. The two stories you told are just the ones that made news. He does kill people. He is drunk, as are most of us. I'm not, because I only drink soda water. He'll not bother you now, but I'll ask you to please take care. Next time you might not be so lucky."

As he spoke, the drinks arrived. He got up.

"Thanks for your help. It's good to see not all his friends are brain-dead like him. It's a pity you weren't there to help him before."

The man sat back down and spoke again to Charli. He opened his jacket slightly for her and she could see the holster with a large calibre handgun.

"I was there, Miss. It was Johnnie's foot on the guy's head. It was, however, me that shot him. After that, I stopped drinking alcohol. Now, please, take care."

He turned away, took Johnnie by the arm and guided him, and the others, away. Jay was full of nervous excitement over this close encounter. She finished her drink quickly and ordered another. As she did so she counselled Charli.

"As he said, Charli, you must be careful. Anything you read, or anything anybody ever tells you, about my country being peaceful and quiet is bullshit. Thailand can be horribly and brutally violent. Trust me on that one. Forget about mai pen rai – that's fucking bullshit. You upset somebody and you'll be beaten up. If they've a knife, you'll be stabbed. If they've a gun, you'll be shot. Most taxi drivers, most lorry drivers, and many of the men who come to places like this have guns. And they're prepared to use them. My father, also…. He's a collection of several. Some legal, others not. He keeps two fully loaded by his bed at all times. I'm very excited about what you did just now. Nearly bloody pissed myself with excitement. But please don't do it again."

Jay's friends had, at first, kept a safe distance from the confrontation. But gradually they drifted over to hear for themselves the story. They had always believed that Jay was exciting to be with. But now, with her new foreign friend, she was even better. First the dress, second the story. All of them knew the politician's son. And all of them wanted the story first-hand so that they could pass it on later to friends who had not been there. So that they could say that they were there, and that they were a part of that evening when the politician's son had finally been humiliated, even though he had not recognised he was being humiliated.

Chapter 3

A few days later, Charli got a call from Jay.

"Hi Charli. Father's having a small party tonight since Oojay got back from up-country. Can you come round? I need the company. I know this may be tough for you. But please, for me, can you do this?"

Charli didn't want to go. She had been dreading this invitation for some time. But Jay did not want to be on her own at this party. And her pleading was convincing, so Charli agreed. Sir John had arrived back in Bangkok from an up-country consultancy the same day and telephoned Charli about an hour later.

"Hello, Charli? I know you're not happy about going to Yai's. But can you do this for Jay? And for me. Please?"

Charli wondered if Jay had detected her reluctance and had asked Sir John to use his charm to persuade her to go as well. Although she had nothing to match Jay's black dress, Charli dressed as daringly as she felt was safe. This was for Jay, as she was certain that Jay would also make a spectacle and would look for moral support.

Charli took the hotel limousine to Yai's mansion off Sukhumvit Road. Sir John had already given the hotel instructions on where to go. As the limousine pulled up outside the imposing compound, Charli felt a sudden unease. There were Mercedes Benzes and BMWs parked outside. The drivers sat smoking and playing Thai chess. Their board was an ancient piece of plywood with faded squares drawn on with a Biro. The pieces were bottle tops. The pawns were made from M-150 or Red Bull tops, rooks were Fanta orange or Green Spot, knights were 7-up or Sprite tops, bishops were Singha or Carlsberg beer tops while the Queens were Coke or Pepsi and the Kings were Mekhong or Saeng Thip. As Charli looked at the board, she thought; *Company battle – Wessel!*

Charli watched them play as the guard at the gate took the taxi driver's ID card. This time, perhaps following on from their recent incident in the discotheque, Charli noted that the guard was armed. But she could not remember from her last visit so assumed that he was armed all the time and she had just not noticed before. He allowed them through. Charli was prepared to walk the one hundred metres and would have preferred to. Instead, the white Volvo drove up to the front of the house.

Charli stepped out. There was no need to go through the embarrassment of paying for the taxi. It was the hotel limousine service and she had put it on her bill. She straightened the expensive purple silk micro-dress and smoothed it down over her purple silk stockings before walking toward the house. To her left, the fountain splashed over almost fifty thousand US dollars' worth of Koi carp. A soft green light shone from below the water. The limousine pulled away, crunching over the gravel as Charli approached the door.

The maid greeted her with downcast eyes. She was dressed beautifully in the traditional northern Thai Lanna style. Her dress was the finest quality Thai silk. Charli immediately sensed Jay's hand in choosing the cloth. To complete the outfit, the maid wore an exquisitely designed silver belt around her waist. She welcomed Charli into the house. They moved to the room where Charli had first met Yai. As Charli entered, she immediately went cold. The room went silent as everyone turned to look at her.

Charli saw that Jay wore a long silk cheongsam. Her hair was tied up and she was wearing a delicate pair of peacock ear-rings in fine gold. Yai was dressed in a smart traditional Thai outfit, as were several other of the men. There were 13 people in the room including Charli. Five were women. Nothing had been said about dress. About what to wear. About what was appropriate or, more importantly, inappropriate. And Charli was dressed inappropriately.

There was one woman in her late thirties who still radiated beauty but was moving towards the middle-aged weight so common of women in Thailand, particularly spoiled Bangkok women. Her face was heavily made up. As Charli looked at her, she realised that if the woman dressed down and wore less make-up, she would still be a beauty. She gave the woman the benefit of the doubt and hoped that the heavy blue eye shadow was only for this evening. Later, she learned that this woman had won the Miss Thailand contest some 20 years ago.

Ex-Miss Thailand was on the arm of a man who was some three inches smaller than her. He was also 35 years older than her. He was General Tem Khrisnaiyataphong. With little public fanfare, he had recently been appointed to the board of KA Holdings. His influence in politics and especially the army could be of great help to KA.

Another woman was in her 40s. She was the wife of Police Colonel Somsak Shinavatranapakdi. Unlike the younger ex-Miss Thailand, this woman was really mutton dressed as mutton. She had a badly-designed silk evening gown that was dripping in unnecessary lace which seemed to merely accentuate her rolls of fat. Around her neck was a large pendant with a garish emerald as its centrepiece. The emerald kept trying to disappear into a fold of her neck and Charli could not help but be hypnotised by its movement. Her fingers were weighted down with equally tasteless rings. She had her hand held out, flashing the baubles and false eyelashes at the younger woman. Emerald Bauble was trying desperately to keep her position in the beauty stakes while all the time falling further behind with the passing years.

Apart from these two, and from Jay and Charli, there was just one other woman in the room. She was tiny. She wore a simple, old-fashioned sarong and blouse. She had, around her neck, a single gold chain with a single diamond. She wore no make-up. But everything about her told Charli that this was a woman with wealth and, more importantly, influence. Looking deep into the old lady's face, Charli also detected a former beauty that still radiated when she smiled.

The old woman had just taken the hand of the mutton but she looked up and smiled at Charli. Charli's eyes were on the old lady as she sat in the one free seat and accepted the drink that Oi - the maid - had automatically brought her. A Campari Soda with fresh lime. As Charli sank into the western style armchair, she hoped that her purple micro-dress would escape the notice of the men in the room. It was a futile hope. Sir John had been talking to the general. He looked at Charli when he realised that the general's gaze was elsewhere.

In the West, most men would have tried to make their stares a little less obvious. The general, however, carried on his conversation with Sir John in Thai, but all the while he stared openly at Charli's purple stocking-clad legs. Charli folded her legs away from him defensively as Jay came over and sat on the arm of the chair. She put her arms around Charli and leaned close to her cheek, kissing her lightly before speaking.

"Oh, thank God you've come. I was going apeshit sitting here without you."

She gave Charli another kiss. Firstly, on the forehead. Secondly, lingeringly, on the lips. Jay pulled slightly away from Charli but still held her face. Charli studied Jay's eyes as the Thai smiled at her and spoke again.

"Thanks Charli."

Rather than carry on her conversation with Charli, Jay sat on the arm of the chair and surveyed the room disapprovingly. A drink was in her right hand. With her left hand she continued to cradle Charli's head, playing idly with her hair while watching the older assemblage. Although mildly uncomfortable at the overt show of affection, Charli allowed the idle grooming to continue. She raised her glass and sipped the Campari. She noticed that the old woman was now holding the soft, fat white palm of the mutton. She was speaking quietly in Thai, gesturing slightly with her delicate fingers as the mutton hung on the old lady's every syllable.

Charli tensed as she realised what this old woman was doing. Jay sensed the change. She caressed Charli's neck, almost massaging her, as she looked down at her friend to see what had startled her.

"Are you okay, Charli?"

Charli looked up at Jay.

"I'm fine."

Charli smiled but unconvincingly.

"I thought this was a dinner party, Jay."

"Oh, no problem, it's a buffet. There's plenty of everything in the kitchen. Oi's been working all day like a slave to make everything. Go when you want. Don't wait for these fat, old, wet farts. They're still talking politics and business. Or is it business and politics? You can never tell when the police and army get together in my country. It'll need a few more Johnnie Walkers and a few more verbal agreements and handshakes before they go for the food. Go and get something now. Maybe you can bring me something. Something farang. I know Oi has made a good mix of farang and Chinese food. But I want farang. Okay? I've had too much bloody MSG for one day. I'm even sweating the stuff now; there're crystals on my skin."

Charli headed to the kitchen. Glad to get away from the gathering of the corrupt. As she approached the quarters where the buffet was laid out, Charli heard quietened voices. Through the open doorway, she saw Sir John and the maid.

In the brightly lit room, Oi was standing with her arms by her side. Sir John's right hand moved to rest lightly on her left shoulder. She instinctively, almost defiantly, pulled her shoulder away. The maid's head and, especially, her eyes were downcast. With his left arm, Sir John was gently pointing a finger in emphasis in front of her face. He spoke quietly in Thai. Charli could not hear what he said, still less understand it. She turned away and went in search of the bathroom.

Charli took a wrong turn and ended up in what she realised was Yai's bedroom. Above the bed was a subtly-lit gun cupboard. On the bedside table were two hand guns left carelessly about with four clips loaded with bullets. She moved quickly to the table and picked up one of the automatics, feeling its weight in the palm of her hand. She placed it back down on the table. Apart from the guns, there was an almost feminine feel to the room. She looked at the black and white print of the naked youth. It was tasteful but disturbing. She left the room and moved on to the bathroom.

Charli did not need to go, but she wanted the time to herself before she went back for the food. She hoped that when she returned, the secret meeting would be over. Charli was confused and could not understand what was happening between Sir John and the maid. One thing, however, was clear to her. The maid wanted nothing to do with Sir John. For one crazy moment, the encounter looked like a problem between two lovers.

She left the bathroom and moved cautiously back to the kitchen, making a deliberate noise as she approached. Sir John smiled at her as she entered the room. He continued to load his plate.

"Come in, Charli, come in. Take some food before the gannets arrive. There's only one thing that'll keep the Thai-Chinese away from demolishing a table of food. And that's serious talk about money. And believe me. Money is always serious to them and they're talking about a lot of money in there."

Charli looked at him as he smiled at her. She held his gaze with her eyes.

"Why am I here, John?"

"Jay didn't want to be alone with this rabble. She wanted your company. Me also. I sometimes get tired of being the 'pet farang'. I often feel like a mascot for Yai. Please don't misunderstand me. I've known him for almost thirty years and he's a good friend. A very old, very dear, and very valued friend. He's done a lot for me. But still… eat some food. Don't look so serious. You've a commanding beauty, Charli, that's enhanced when you smile. That dress also helps. In spite of what you may think, it was a wonderful choice for this evening. I know of two women who now hate you and several men who adore you. And that's as it should be. It's a natural order for the world."

With this last comment, he moved back into the main room.

Charli filled two plates with food for herself and for Jay. As she did so, she noticed Oi watching her and as she filled her plate, she looked at the maid. Far more beautiful, and regal, than the mutton in the other room. But, nevertheless, waiting upon them.

Oi spoke to Charli for the first time.

"Miss Charli, I see you before. Don't worry. When you see me and Doctor John, he is helping me with some problem. Doctor John stay in this family many years now - me also. He knows many things about this family. He is good man."

Charli was surprised at the quality of the maid's English. Not comparable to Jay's, but still far superior to many that she had heard. For the first time, the maid smiled at Charli. She nodded her head.

"I'm thinking you know that. He's a very good man. Not like the Thai man. There're many things he can do for people and many things he cannot do. But I know always he tries very hard for everybody. He is not always succeeding. Many times he fail. For this failing I know always he has the tired heart. But I know he tries. That is his heart. And for this reason, I know Doctor John is good man."

"Many Thai man say they are Buddhist. But there is no man I see with a Buddhist heart. No Thai man. Doctor John tells me many times he is not Buddhist. He say he is not Christian also. But I know his heart. He has the heart on the right path. It not got there yet. But it going in the right way. Doctor John not have to go to temple and make merit to be a good Buddhist."

She smiled again at Charli. Charli looked at the woman who had never spoken to her before. She looked out of the kitchen and back toward the room where distant voices were being raised in laughter. Charli was about to speak to the maid when two figures moved out of the doorway and into the kitchen.

General Tem and Police Colonel Somsak entered the kitchen. They glared at Charli as they continued speaking in Thai. Embarrassed to speak to her because their English was not as good as Jay's or Yai's or even that of the Isan maid. And suddenly, acknowledging the presence of the maid, they switched their discussion from Thai to Chinese. They started on the buffet as Charli left the kitchen. Charli looked back once at the maid and was startled by the barely disguised look of loathing on her face. When Charli entered the lounge, she was surprised to see that Jay had taken the seat next to the old lady. Charli tensed. Jay looked up.

"Charli. My food. Thanks. Come here and sit with Grandma Djim. She wants to meet you."

Charli moved cautiously towards the old lady. She had no option but to sit next to her. She gave the food to Jay. The old lady turned to Charli. This was the first clear view that she had of Charli. She gasped in surprise when she saw Charli's face. *She saw her long-lost daughter.* Jay glanced at the old lady but relaxed when she saw the look of surprise evaporate quickly.

"My son said you were very beautiful, but he didn't tell me how beautiful. You remind me... of someone I met at a party. A long time ago."

The old lady smiled at Charli. She had a presence that was unmatched in the house except by one other person. Charli had not, again, expected such perfect English from such an old lady as this. Having never been a colony, the Thais were still playing catch up with the English language. The old lady turned to Jay and berated her in English.

"Jitta, you're a bad influence on Charli. You should've told her your father expected this to be a polite dinner. I know that Charli's not happy dressing so indecorously. She did this for you. I know also that Charli would've dressed otherwise if you'd alerted her beforehand. Charli's a good girl, Jitta. You're not."

As she said this, she was wagging a delicate, bony finger at Jay.

"You should think more, Jitta. Think. You're very clever. You've had a good education in England. The best. But there're times when you don't think. Only for yourself. Only for what you want. Sometimes, many times, your selfishness makes you stupid."

As the old lady did this, she prodded her finger against the forehead of the chastened Jay.

She turned to Charli and smiled. Charli could not help but smile back. Charli put her plate down on the grey-pink coffee table made from imported Italian Dolomite. As she did this, Jay picked up Charli's drink, which she had brought over. She raised it in front of Charli and gave it to her.

"I'm sorry Charli. I should've warned you. I didn't think. Grandma Djim's right. As ever."

Charli, from what she had learned of Jay, had expected sarcasm in this statement. She saw that Jay's eyes had watered slightly at the embarrassment she had caused. There was genuine respect for the old lady. But a respect that was different to that which she showed her father. Jay smiled at her grandmother.

"I hadn't thought to warn you that father was expecting formal dress."

She then looked at Grandma Djim and lightened up.

"However. What you're wearing is causing a sensation. Hia Tem can't keep his beady, reptilian eyes off your legs."

Charli was surprised as Grandma Djim slapped Jay across the thigh. The tension was broken as Charli realised it was playful.

"Oh, come on GeeDee. You hate him as much as I do."

The old lady turned to Charli.

"Do you see what I mean? I'm sorry Charli. Jay was very impolite, as usual. In Thailand it's not good to refer to a general of the armed forces as a lizard - Hia. Education in England has given her bad manners. Very bad manners. She has no respect for seniority. She has no respect for authority. Look how she treats me; with the same feelings as for a temple dog. My brain is bruised from the mental kicking she gives me every day. That's all I'm good for. To be kicked around like a temple dog."

At once Charli could see that this was not true and that Jay plainly had immense respect for the old lady. She could also see that, despite what she had been saying, the old lady knew this. There was a closeness between the two that transcended the generations. Charli could also see that the old lady shared the same loathing for Hia Tem that Jay had. Separated by a generation or two, they appeared to have so much in common. Relaxed, as she realised the other people in the room were being reduced to a side-show, Charli turned to the old lady and spoke.

"I think, Grandma Djim, that Jay's got a lot of respect for you. She certainly has a lot of love for you."

"Ha. She's a funny way to show it. If you love me so much, Jay, why is my glass empty? Fill it, girl. And don't get me any of that Johnnie Walker rubbish the army 'elite' is drinking. Laphroaig. You know I like Laphroaig."

Jay got up and moved to the drinks cabinet. The old lady continued speaking with Charli.

"These men sit and throw back their Johnnie Walker Black Label while planning their next campaign, Charli. Fools, Charli. The lot of them."

She fell silent. Charli looked at her face in the shadows. Jay arrived with a fresh drink for the old lady – the 40-year-old Laphroaig. She also gave an identical glass of whisky to Charli to go with her Campari Soda. Charli looked at her quizzically. Jay nodded back at Charli. It was suddenly clear to Charli that Jay had realised the importance of the conversation between the two. Charli had never tasted Laphroaig before. But this was given to her to stimulate, or generate, empathy between her and the old lady. The atmosphere of the room changed. All others disappeared. Even Jay became just a peripheral observer to the old lady and Charli.

The old lady took a sip from the small glass. No ice. Only the whisky from the island of Islay. She closed her eyes. Charli watched her and then took a drink. The taste of peat and a myriad of other flavours warmed her mouth. The old lady exhaled a slight breath. Still with her eyes closed, she spoke.

"Have you ever been to the island Charli? Islay is so very beautiful. And cold. I was just 23. It was 1937. I leave it to you to work out how old I am now. A magical island. Did you know that Laphroaig means 'beautiful hollow by the broad bay' in Scottish Gaelic? A magical language but one I could never master, alas."

She opened her eyes and turned her head to Charli and continued.

"I was so young, Charli, and there was so very much for me to look forward to. My country was prospering. The 'Rice Bowl of Asia'. My family was prospering. We were, after all, rice merchants. In 1937, nobody could guess what Hitler and the Japanese had in mind. I'd been in England for nearly five years. Studying."

She closed her eyes and sipped at the whisky again. Charli did likewise. Jay looked on. She had never heard Grandma Djim speak like this before. Certainly not with someone she was meeting for the first time. And certainly not with a foreigner. With her eyes closed, the old lady smiled as she travelled back some sixty years in time.

"But mostly going to parties. Far more fun than studying, don't you agree? You must be curious about my English, Charli. I know you have been curious as to how an old lady such as I could speak such good English. It helps that I lived in England for several years. But also, most importantly. I had some excellent teachers. Mister Winston Churchill among them, as he then was."

She opened her eyes and smiled at Charli who was open-mouthed at what the Grandma Djim was saying. There were raised voices in the background. The general and police colonel had returned with their food. Torn back to the present, Charli glanced briefly at them and noticed they had begun to shuffle food noisily into their mouths with chopsticks, chomping away at the food like animals on a farm. As

Charli glanced at them, she saw that the general was watching her. And she knew which parts of her body he was watching. Charli turned her back to him. The old lady spoke again.

"October, 1938, Charli, my family were invited to Chartwell. Mister Winston's home. I was young. Maybe the same as you. Maybe a little older. You're? 23? 24??"

"Twenty-three."

Charli sipped her drink and was surprised that it had almost gone. With equal surprise, she noted that Grandma Djim had also finished her drink. Jay got up immediately and went to replenish the glasses. As she did so, a tinny voice trilled from across the room. It was Hia Tem.

"Jay. Whi' you there. Get Black Label for me, Choo also. Plenty ice. And maybe you talk your father sack the maid. I not see the lazy Laos-Isan sow do anything all evening. I don't know why he keep her. She is old, scrawny like chicken, and ugly."

Charli looked at Grandma Djim. Grandma Djim merely shrugged her shoulders.

Jay took the drinks to the two men and then looked after Grandma Djim, Charli, and herself. Jay rarely drank Laphroaig. But now, drifting into the past with Charli and Grandma Djim, she felt compelled to join them with the drink. The three entered a different universe. It involved a spiritual unification that all of the modern 20th century had failed to overcome.

"I was 24, nearly 25, Charli. I didn't want to go. So many old people."

She creased her forehead. Almost in disgust.

"So very old. Mister Winston? Pompous, fat, and drunk. As usual.

Smelling of cigars. As usual. In his 60s. Old, Charli, so old."

The 80-year-old lady grinned at the absurdity of this comment.

"I know how you're feeling Charli. I was the same. There are some, Charli, who cannot be changed by time. On the outside, Charli, yes. We're all, every one of us, changed. Look at me. Wasted now with age. That's the way of God. Or whatever. Whomever. But inside? No. Not always. There are some who can't be changed. A precious few. I see me in you, Charli. I sense you in me. Open your eyes and open your heart. You'll see me in you as well. You'll sense me in you as well. In your future, when I'm returned to dust."

Charli was stung. She put the glass down on the dolomite table and picked at some food. She felt a tenseness in her stomach. A pain which stabbed, a pain like nothing she had never felt before. Jay looked sharply at Charli. She noticed the muscle twitch in her neck. Charli tried to consider how this old lady with her high society connections could ever feel she had anything in common with her. A single word flashed through Charli's mind.

Impossible.

The old lady continued.

"Chartwell, 1938. I was bored. So very bored. I didn't want to go. There were so many men with stuffed shirts. My father had been invited, and I came along for the colour. Everyone told me how beautiful I was. I was the 'Oriental Pet' just as you're now the 'Farang Pet'. Something, a flower, an object of beauty, to be admired by all. Like you at this party. I was beautiful, Charli. You may not believe, now, how beautiful I was."

Charli looked hard at the old lady. Even in her 80s, the old lady gave off an aura of beauty that age could not dim.

"I can believe it. Grandma Djim. I can believe it. If you've some pictures of yourself in the past I'd like to see those. Please."

The old lady lifted her hand to Charli's cheek.

"Another time. There should be other times. That evening, Charli, everything changed. Before then, I'd believed the world was safe and I was safe. I'd read little about the world. Why should I? In 1938, girls, especially Asian girls, weren't expected to know the complexity of the affairs of the world. That was the domain of a man. But that evening, Charli, I listened. To all the old men. But especially to Mister Winston."

"Mister Winston was railing against his government. I think he'd been drinking too much brandy. As usual. Chamberlain had recently returned from Munich. He was basking in the glory of a nation grateful for the promised peace which he had extracted from Hitler. All the old men listened to Mister Winston. Mister Winston mocked 'peace for our time'. They laughed. He told somebody who scoffed at him that he deserved everything that was about to rain down.

They ate his food, Charli. They drank his fine wines, his fine whisky, and his fine brandy. They smoked his fine La Aroma de Cuba cigars. They listened and they laughed. My father also. I didn't know the man. But one turned and spoke to Mister Winston. To this day Charli I remember what he said. Not the words. But the thought.

He told Mister Winston that he'd been coming out with the same paranoia for more than seven years. He told everybody in the room that Germany was less of a threat, now, with a failed artist in charge, than it had been in the days of Bismarck. That man looked directly at me, Charli, as he said that Hitler was probably the best thing that could happen to Germany, and certainly the best thing to happen to Europe. He told Mister Winston that, thanks to Hitler, Germany was now reduced to being a neutered lapdog of the French.

Mister Winston went quiet. He got up to make himself a fresh drink. As he passed me I heard him mutter 'some lapdog'."

Chapter 4

For Charli, the room was far away now. It felt like the voices were in the distance. There was also some laughter. But for her, this felt as if it was from another room. Certainly, it was from another time. Charli was now sitting in the library at Chartwell. The potent smell of cigar smoke drifted in front of her as the portly figure of Winston Churchill stopped beside her.

Thin wisps of cigar smoke drifted into her face and stung her eyes. She coughed involuntarily, delicately holding her left hand in front of her mouth.

"This must be very boring for you, my dear. Old men reminiscing about battles past and dreaming about battles new. I'm sorry that Sarah could not be here to give you some small piece of her company. There's a tradition in our world that after dinner the ladies should retire separately. Your father wished otherwise for you. I'm most terribly sorry."

"However, I see you're drinking my Laphroaig. The first lady, as I recall, to drink Laphroaig at Chartwell. And the first Burmese lady, for certain, to visit Chartwell. Congratulations my dear. So many firsts in one evening for one so young."

"Burma is a most special, and important, country for the Empire. I can assure you that Burma will grow, as you must grow with her, to have a most fruitful future. But for this to happen, my dear, you have to help me persuade the imbecile assemblage here tonight that the future holds no security for any unless we all take some action against Hitler and his brigands. Do you think you can do that? Do you think you can help an old man such as I to convince these fools that unless they open their eyes soon that everything will change? And change, believe me, for the bad. Not for the good."

Mister Winston Churchill smiled at the fragile Burmese beauty perched nervously on the edge of her seat. Her heart had fluttered at the first meeting with such a famous, but now, finally, fallen man. Before going to the party, her father had told her of this man whose glories were all now in the past. So sad. Churchill moved away and was slapped on the back by an anonymous Tory minister. A minister who had never liked him. A minister who was glad when Winston Churchill had left the Conservative party and sorry when he had returned. A minister who had always regarded Winston Churchill 'a maverick unrequired by His Majesty's subjects'.

Grandma Djim turned to Charli as Charli spoke.

"I'm sorry. I didn't know you were Burmese. I assumed you were Thai."

The old lady laughed.

"Oh, don't worry my dear. To farang we must all look the same. You probably couldn't tell the difference between me, a Mongolian, or a Cherokee Indian. But what is Thai? I'm Burmese. But that's only the surface. In the past, my family was a powerful Chinese family in Burma. Hia? Chinese. Somsak-Choo? Chinese. Their bloated wives or mistresses? Chinese, Chinese. Truth be told, Charli. I think the only true Thai in this house is Oi, the maid. Her line is very pure. I see no Chinese in her."

"My country, Charli, was a colony of England. A part of Mister Winston's 'Empire'. All of the countries of southern Asia belonged, at one time or another, to European powers. All that is except for one. Siam - as it was. Thailand - as it is. But Thailand, like every country in Southeast Asia, has been controlled by another colonial power; China. What does not make this so obvious to a white man is the colour of our skin. But believe me, if Hitler had got his way, you'd be speaking German, working in the kitchen, like Oi, and cursing your German masters in much the same way as Oi curses her Chinese masters."

The old lady was speaking a truth that was getting close to a reality that Charli did not want to confront. At least just yet. Her thoughts went back briefly to Lek and some of the things Lek had said to her. Lek, whose world had been a lot further away from this evening than this was from Chartwell. She arose and went to the kitchen on the pretext of looking for some food.

Charli stood staring at the destruction on the table that had been waged by the men out of uniform. She felt an arm over her shoulders and turned to face Jay, who was smiling sympathetically at her.

"I'm sorry Charli. I know you didn't want to come here. I didn't either. But there're some things even I feel obliged to do. You okay? You looked as if you'd seen a ghost or something when Grandma Djim was speaking to you. I saw the tic in your neck. I see it often when you're tense. It's quite hypnotic. You should patent it some time. I notice things like that. She didn't mean any of it, I'm sure."

Charli put down the food she had picked up.

"Jay, I want to go back to my hotel now. I think that'd be best."

Jay nodded at her.

"Please, don't get me wrong. I like your Grandma Djim. She's a fascinating lady. But I'm not in the right frame of mind for this at the moment. Not after the events of the last few weeks. Please understand, I lost a very dear friend recently. I'll go and make my goodbyes to Grandma Djim. Maybe I can see her in the future. I'd like to. But not now, okay?"

They moved back to the lounge. Charli stopped Jay at the door. The tic was playing in her neck and Jay's eyes were drawn, inexorably, to the slight pulse.

"Oh, and Jay. She did mean it. She meant, and she believed, every word she spoke to me. I don't know how she knows about my life. But she knows. And that frightens me, that frightens me a lot."

Jay appeared confused. She stared at Charli, and suddenly she realised that Charli was not of her world. In an instant she realised that there was a vast gulf between herself and Charli. A gulf only matched by that between herself and her one other true friend, Grandma Djim. Jay had little respect for those about her. There were, however, three people she did respect. The maid, Sir John - her 'uncle' - and Grandma Djim. And now, she realised, a fourth was added because Charli was the same as Grandma Djim.

They walked back into the room and Jay was left puzzled by Charli's last statement. She had heard Uncle John refer to the 'Enigmatic Charli' before. But this had always been in the form of a joke. Now she was not so sure it was a joke.

After the party, Charli sat in her hotel room for an hour or more. She drank more whisky and listened to the air-conditioning. She wondered when she would meet the old lady again. She had to. Many thoughts were going through her head as she tried to recall all that had been said that evening. That night she had a disturbed sleep waking many times. Lek and the white tiger returned. Always the same dream but with minor, though important, variations.

Chapter 5

Charli and Jay arranged to meet some days later. As Jay entered the restaurant, heads turned and voices muttered. She bounced over to Charli's table with a broad smile, knowing that she was now, once again, the centre of attention. Charli looked at her disapprovingly as she sat down. Jay smiled at Charli and turned to look over her shoulder.

"Ignore them, Charli. They're all so fucking stuck up. I feel sorry for them, don't you?"

Charli did not feel sorry for the people in the restaurant. She felt sorry for Jay for continuing to insist on making a fool of herself in this way. This time she had arrived in a plastic, red micro-mini with a brief white crop top that exposed her midriff. It was also clear that she had chosen not to wear a bra. Not that she really needed to.

Charli remembered back to a single occasion when she had been berated by a 20-year-old go-go dancer from Patpong for dressing 'inappropriately'. Charli had taken Lek to a discotheque and had worn a figure-hugging grey light-wool minidress with no bra or knickers. Charli had tried to explain to Lek that the whole effect of the minidress would have been ruined had the lines of bra and knickers been visible. Lek's simple, and strangely logical reply was that if that was the case, then the dress should not be worn.

"Maybe in your country, Charli, farang-lady can make like this. In Thailand no. Cannot make like this. Not good. You understand me. Not polite."

As Charli got to know Lek more and more, she learned many lessons in Thai etiquette from the young prostitute. She related this story to Jay. But it was lost on the Roedean-educated woman.

The manager of the restaurant came over to their table and spoke quietly with Jay. She was polite to him. When he had gone, she translated for Charli, although from the tone of the discussion, Charli had already gathered what was being said.

Jay's father was well known and respected in this particular hotel. However, the management could not look lightly upon the style of dress that Jay had chosen to wear. The management had noted that had this been anybody else, she would have been immediately asked to leave. The management further noted that seeing as this was Miss Jittawadee, she would be requested to contain her movements in the restaurant, finish her business with her foreign friend and to then leave as unobtrusively as possible. The management further requested that the next time Miss Jittawadee considered coming to the hotel, she should dress in a manner more appropriate for that hotel.

Charli counselled Jay.

"There're times and places, Jay, when it's possible to make fashion statements. As much as I admire your sense of adventure, I find myself in agreement with the management. Call me stuck-up if you wish. Have you considered what people may think of me? It was difficult enough in the past trying to find suitable places to take Lek to. Although she was a go-go dancer, she never gave anything away to suggest she was. She always dressed smartly – conservatively even."

"But don't you see, Charli. She had to dress smartly. She was an up-country girl and everyone in the restaurants that you go to would see that. It didn't matter how she dressed. They'd still think the same of your friend. One look at her dark skin, flattened nose, her 'Isan features', would've been enough. They'd label her immediately as working in an unwholesome business. If she was dressed smartly and going to a restaurant with a farang, male or female, it was certain she wasn't a maid. And if she wasn't a maid, people would assume, then, that she worked in the 'entertainment' industry. It's that simple. I'm sorry, I didn't make the rules."

Charli snorted lightly at this. Remembering back to some of her experiences when taking Lek out, she knew, however, that Jay was right.

"I'm sorry, Charli. This is Thailand. Or more importantly, this is Bangkok. Not every Thai looks the same. I've never met your friend, Lek. But I bet she had northern features and a darker complexion than me."

Charli studied Jay's features and nodded.

"Not just in Thailand, Charli. It's the same in your country. The girls at my school all had features that came from the good breeding stock of the British, no English, upper classes. Not like you. But in Britain, there's now less emphasis on class. A little less anyway. If they want to see true class separation, they should come to my country, Charli. Come to Thailand. And then they'll see what class and racial differences, racism, xenophobia even, are really about. Ours is an apartheid society."

"In Thailand, there's still so much emphasis on family. On breeding. And I'm not sure if that'll change. At least no time soon. Your friend, Lek, would always have been regarded as a poor northerner. Just like Oi, our maid. She'd never have found a rich Thai to marry. Especially in Patpong. Her only chance was to find a caring farang to look after her. But I can tell you; If she'd found that man and if they'd lived in Thailand, she would've had to spend the rest of her life being looked down on as a bar girl. Even if she hadn't been. Stigmatised because of who she was and who she'd chosen to marry. Welcome to my country, Charli. The Japanese have much to learn when it comes to xenophobia. South Africans also. They're mere amateurs. We've, the Chinese-Thai especially, perfected the art of xenophobia to a level where you don't even realise it's taking place. Beat that if you can."

"Okay, Charli, I'm sorry for the way I've dressed. Maybe I wasn't thinking so well. As usual. That's me, haha. But can you understand why I've done this? Believe it or not, I want to change things in my country. I don't like this fucking attitude."

"Yes, I went to an expensive school in Britain. But one thing it did was make me more aware that breeding and class aren't important. At that school, I met some real bitches. Politically, I met some who professed to being Tory, some socialist. I've a lot of sympathy now for socialism. It's no longer necessary in your country. It's necessary in mine - if only to bring about social change. That's why I don't like the military in my country. They're frightened of change. Because in change they see a loss of power for them."

"In my country, the military become politicians. And they buy their votes from families in the provinces. Families like Lek's. The last thing they want is for Lek and her kind - her sisters and her brothers, her sons and her daughters - to be educated."

"Oh sure, Charli. They talk of it. Chart Thai, Chart Pattana. All controlled by ex-military. But the last thing they want is for their voters to wake up one day and say 'Hey, we've been conned'."

Despite Jay's excellent education, Charli had not really considered how bright she was. But as she listened to her speak, she knew that here was somebody who thought about, and cared for, her country. Unlike the military and the politicians. Men who thought about, and cared for, only themselves.

"Your friend Lek and me must've been very different. I don't have to tell you that, Charli. But I bet there were some things that made us the same. I bet we both had a deep respect for our country, our King, and our religion. My education's now given me the chance to question our politicians and our military. I've no respect for them. I've no respect for their money. The way it was gathered. By being

the biggest, fattest pig in the sty. And that's an insult to pigs."
"How do you think most of the army got their wealth? Drug-trafficking, that's how. I know that father's never been involved, but he knows many who were and he knows many who still are. Why do you think he sleeps with a gun? I could name a dozen politicians who are still actively involved. That shit we met at the Forbidden City last week. How do you think his father got so wealthy? Drugs, Charli. That's one thing I'll say for Johnnie Walker, at least. He's not involved in drugs, he's too bloody stupid."

"When father has these evenings, I'm bored and have little to do but listen and be the pretty ornament. These men talk brazenly of their deals. Do you know how much heroin passes through Thailand every year? I'll tell you – more than 300,000 kilogrammes. That's nearly 1,000 kilos every single day. I know for sure that Somsak - Choo - is involved. Do you think drugs could pass easily through the country if it weren't for the help of the police or the army? It is, ironically, probably the most carefully controlled and well-managed business in my country. Even today."

"You know our party the other week? Father laid that on for Choo and Tem. They were sorting out a large shipment that's about to go off. Why do you think Tem's just been brought on to the board of KA Holding? Because of his influence. He rose through the ranks in the northern border areas during the sixties. This was when the American CIA were financing their 'secret war' in Laos by drug running. Thirty years on they're all still at it. The same old bloody game, Charli."

"Do you know what's the most important diplomatic posting for Thailand? Japan? America? Germany? Certainly not the UK. It's Switzerland. Ask yourself why? Whoever runs the Swiss Embassy is able to act as banker for all the drug smugglers. Think about it. Numbered bank accounts. No names."

"I don't know if your friend ever questioned these institutions. The military and the government."

Jay took a drink.

"My country's obsessed with appearance. Not like in the West. Have you seen some of the women walking around the supermarkets, Charli? They look as if they're about to attend a bloody cocktail evening. It's pathetic. All for show. And all they're doing is the bloody daily shopping."

"I've dressed for show today. But I've dressed in something that I'm comfortable wearing. Maybe my choice was inappropriate today. But no less inappropriate than some of the tacky cocktail dresses you can see being worn by Bangkok's nouveau riche as they swan around Central supermarket with their trolley, mobile telephone, and Pomeranian."

Charli had seen these flowers of fashion herself. And she agreed with Jay that they did look pathetic.

The following day, Charli met Jay in the lobby of her hotel. They had not decided where to go for the evening. As usual, Charli had come down early. As usual, Jay had little respect for time and arrived thirty minutes late. In the meantime, Steven Hunt appeared.

"Charli, what a pleasant surprise. You're still in Bangkok. You should've contacted me so we could arrange something."

Charli disguised her true feelings at meeting him. She smiled thinly.

"I'm sorry Steven. I knew you'd returned to Bangkok. The hotel keeps me well-informed of your movements. I'm with a friend."

"Have you forgotten your promise? You said you'd take me to Khao Yai some time. Don't let me down now. I'm looking forward to this trip. Like you, I need to get out of Bangkok on a regular basis. KA pay me well for my consultancy but they demand almost every minute of my day. I'd really welcome a trip out of town. Honestly."

As he spoke these words, Jay arrived. Charli gasped slightly as she saw Jay enter the lobby bar in a figure-hugging, light-wool dress. Steven Hunt turned and could not keep his eyes from Jay's body. Before Charli could say anything, Jay had sat down and, along the way, attracted the attention of a waiter. This, in itself, had not been difficult. She spoke to him in English.

"Do you have Laphroaig? I want a Laphroaig for me, Singha beer for Miss Charli, and...?"

She looked at Hunt with a raised eyebrow.

"Glenfiddich for me, thank you."

The waiter went away, only to return a few minutes later. As Jay had spoken English to him, he spoke English to her. He assumed she was Filipina.

"Sorry Miss. Laphroaig no have."

Jay uttered a solitary expletive and ordered, instead, a Singha beer. She then changed the order.

"No, make that a Glenfiddich. Two Glenfiddichs."

Steven introduced himself to Jay.

"Hello, I'm Steven Hunt. And if I can say, Charli's girlfriends get more beautiful at every encounter."

He took Jay's hand and kissed it lightly on the back.

The three exchanged some pleasantries, during which Jay learned a little of Hunt and he learned a little of her. He rapidly reached the conclusion that Jay was a new partner for Charli Harris. The way that Jay idly massaged Charli's neck only reinforced this belief. A replacement for Lek. He wondered, however, where Charli had found Jay. Jay appeared far more educated and sophisticated than the simple bar girl. Hunt sipped his drink while occasionally looking at his watch. He was aware that he was in the middle of a pre-arranged meeting, and he felt slightly embarrassed. He finished his drink quickly.

"I'm sorry, ladies, I have to go. An already arranged meeting. Please, Charli, don't forget your promise to take me to Khao Yai."

Jay came alive.

"Khao Yai? Oh wow. It's maybe ten years since I've been. Can I come too, Charli?"

Charli glanced quickly at Jay.

"I'm sorry, Jay, this is something special I've promised Steven for a long time. I'll take you another time."

At these words, Hunt realised he had finally broken through. He felt pleased with himself as he made his apologies and left. Also at these words, Jay looked at Charli. Charli, she knew, had bad-mouthed Hunt for as long as Jay had known her.

CHAPTER 6

Charli received a message from Grandma Djim asking to meet her for lunch. They met at a downtown hotel that Grandma Djim had chosen. The name of the hotel was not familiar to Charli; it was not one of Bangkok's better-known hotels. Small but exclusive, it was owned by Grandma Djim and prided itself on avoiding the many guide books about Thailand. As Charli entered the restaurant, she was not sure how to ask for the table. But then she saw the old lady sitting in a corner with a commanding view of the entire room. Charli sat opposite her with her back to the restaurant.

"Thank you for coming, Charli. I've wanted to talk with you for some time but was unable to before now. Jitta seems to monopolise so much of your free time now. That's as it should be as you're the same age. I apologise for the appalling behaviour of my son's acquaintances the other week. And also for Jitta. But surrounded by these people and given her education, I think you can understand how it is that Jitta reacts the way she does at times. She's frivolous but her heart is good. I'm counting on you to correct her Charli. I can't do this. I'm an old lady. And alas. In today's society, Jitta rarely listens to me. But you're also an old lady in many ways, I know this. You have a wisdom and maturity that's far beyond your years. There is therefore much you can teach Jitta and she'll listen because she doesn't see you as I do."

Charli interrupted the old lady.

"Grandma Djim, please, Jay's got a lot of respect for you, I know that. And I know she listens and learns from you more than you may think. Furthermore, there's no need to patronise me. If you knew anything of me you'd understand I've no real wisdom."

The old lady smiled and nodded dismissively at Charli's statement. But she was careful to note that Charli had not questioned her use of the word maturity. Charli continued.

"Your country, your adopted country, is changing so quickly. Changes which, in the past, took several generations to develop are now taking place within a generation. It must be very difficult for Jay to appreciate and to adapt. I don't think I could handle it. One thing I know for sure, and that's that Jay has no respect for the police, for the military, or for the politicians. She's no respect for their corruption. But that's not a bad thing. That's why she doesn't like her father's friends. And I must also say; I wasn't happy with them the other week either. Their kind, Thai, English, or whatever, sicken me."

"But Jay's indicated to me how much she respects you. Don't worry about Jay, Grandma Djim. She's a good girl. As you said, frivolous and immature, but with a good heart."

At this last sentence, the old lady looked up at Charli.

"Unlike you Charli. Mature beyond your years. She's 22-years-old. But you're right, she sometimes acts like a spoilt little teenager."

Charli corrected the old lady.

"All the time. It's something I've noticed, Grandma Djim. In Thailand, women who've had a smothered and protected life are very immature. How else can you explain women in their 30s putting fluffy toys in the backs of their cars or carrying about fluffy rats dressed up in outfits?"

Grandma Djim laughed.

"Yes, many of our women are spoiled and over-protected. And I detest this fashion for carrying toy dogs about in bags and dressing them up like babies."

Charli talked about her friend Lek. Smothered maybe, but by a father who lacked the resources to give her the protection that she needed. She suggested that girls from poor families have to grow up quickly and therefore have more maturity than the pampered princesses of Thailand's high society and middle classes. Grandma Djim agreed.

"So, how is it you're so mature Charli? You told me you lacked wisdom. But you didn't question my observation of your maturity. You're clearly comfortably well off and yet you don't fit the picture you've just painted."

"There're always exceptions to the rules, Grandma Djim. I grew up quickly. Too quick."

The old lady smiled at Charli's evasion.

"Of course. You're young. The same age, nearly, as Jitta - Jay. Whatever she wishes to call herself. I could never have a conversation like this with Jitta. She's too capricious - too wrapped up in her MTV culture. But not you. I was right when I first saw you. Can I see your hands, please?"

The old lady smiled as she held out her hands to take hold of Charli's. Charli moved her hands across the table. Her fingers touched the old lady's just as the old lady continued to speak.

"It's possible to learn so much about a person from their hands. From reading their palms."

With these words, it was as if something had electrocuted Charli. She rapidly pulled her hands back, clenching her fists as she hid them beneath the table.

"Oh. I'm sorry Charli. I hadn't realised. In Thailand, almost everybody likes to have their palms read. It's very important for people, especially for us Chinese. But also many Thai people, many farang as well, are happy for me to read their palms. I hadn't thought you'd object. Please forgive me."

"People look for guidance for their future by having their palms read. Especially when read by somebody with age and wisdom such as I've accumulated. Some won't make a major decision unless they consult a person like myself. With humility, I must say I've guided the fortunes of many over the years. Two prime ministers no less. I'll give away no secrets by noting that much of it's to do with interpreting an accumulated knowledge. There's no real magic."

Charli felt stung as she glared at the old lady who suddenly appeared to her like one of the witches that had taunted her early life in the almost forgotten readings of horrible fairy tales that she had never wanted to listen to. She remembered back to those readings. She remembered a six-year-old girl running from the group reading and being beaten for her bad behaviour. From then on, she had regarded that teacher as a witch.

A young Charli had stared sullenly at the witch at the front of the classroom, trying to make her black heart, coursing with black blood, stop beating with the power of her thoughts. She hated the other girls who laughed at 'Stupid Charlotte'. Scared of a silly story. And afterwards Charli had sat on her own and nursed her friend, Bo-Bo. The teddy bear she would talk to in the night. Until she fell asleep to dream of witches in the dark forest.

Whatever happened to Bo-Bo?

As this sudden flash of an almost forgotten memory passed over her, Charli recovered and looked across at Grandma Djim.

"No, please, Grandma Djim. Will you forgive me? I don't want to have my palms read because I don't want to see my future. I want it to be a surprise. It's much more interesting that way."

As she said this, Grandma Djim looked deep into Charli's eyes. And she could see that she was lying. It was not the future that concerned Charli, it was the past. The old lady could sense this deeply. And if she could have looked at Charli's hands, she could have learned so much about her past. But it was not to be. She did not press matters further. She knew she had made the right choice because she had only seen such torment in a soul once before. When she looked in a mirror many years ago. Another life ago.

"I'm not some kind of ogre, Charli. I'm not a witch. But many people do believe there's some truth in palm-reading. It's a major industry in the far east. Not just the Gypsy fortune tellers seated at the end of your rusting Victorian piers. I'm quite fascinated by your character Charli. In my 80 years, I've rarely... I'll rephrase that... I've never come across somebody like you. You're destined to fulfil an important act, that I know. You can ignore my counsel if you want, but please listen to me for now and indulge an old lady. You can't ignore your destiny. Your Karma. Remember, I'm a Buddhist. You may be as well. I know you're not Christian."

How do you know I'm not Christian?

She held up her hand to still any words from Charli. She continued speaking.

"It's not the future that scares you, Charli. It's your past. I know you've a good life now. You must have money to be able to travel so freely in Thailand without the need of a stifling job - you're lucky. Think about that. You don't need to be a palm-reader to see this. But something troubles you and you should let it go. Dismiss it like a breeze in the night. A burp. A fart. Whatever. But dismiss it. It's the past, and the past is no longer important. You should accept your present and develop it into the future. I know this because I'm the same as you. I only truly found my peace when I put the horrors of my past behind me and reached for my future."

You're 23. Carry your life forward to my age and put your current past, whatever it is, into that perspective. Whatever happened, and for however long that it happened, will seem like a distant memory when you're 80 like me. Events that seem so important now will become less so with time. Believe me, I know this."

"And as I near the end of my life, I think you must agree I've not done so very badly. My son's not perfect, far from it. But he's successful and he looks after me. What more could an aged widow wish for? And he looks after Jitta as best he can. It wasn't easy for Yai without a wife. But Jitta has done quite well with my help and with the help of Oi. And also, always, with the help of John. This is my family, Charli. But Jay needs a woman's touch."

Charli interrupted Grandma Djim to apologise.

"I'm sorry that I suggested that you smothered Jay."

"Don't be sorry. You're right. Like so many girls of her generation, she's had such an easy life that she's been able to remain a child for too long. Far too long. She hasn't been through what you and I have seen. Don't apologise Charli. I was like her at that age. I told you a few weeks ago about my oh-so-perfect life in England. My meeting with Mister Winston Churchill. I was no different from Jitta. Frivolous, capricious."

"But you changed?"

"Yes, Charli. I was changed. With the start of World War II, my family decided to move me back to the safety of Burma. Away from Hitler's ghastly bombs. I married my English love in early 1940. I was 26. By the end of 1940, I had two beautiful babies. Twins. A boy and a girl. And by the end of 1941, I'd added a third to a perfect family. Another boy. December of 1941 was very beautiful in my country.

The cool season was perfect for the Christmas festivities in Rangoon, where we had a beautiful house overlooking the Inle Lake. And the European war seemed so very unimportant and, importantly, so far away. So very far away."

Grandma Djim laughed nervously and reached across to hold Charli's hand as she reminisced about this. Charli was wary of the ploy but decided it impolite to pull her hand away as she had instinctively wanted to do. Grandma Djim sensed the conflict. She continued to hold the young woman's hand but proceeded no further with her examination. As she continued to speak, she toyed lightly with the torn skin around Charli's fingernails. She studied Charli's hands as surreptitiously as she could but proceeded no further out of respect. She knew one thing about Charli, she had a powerful Karma. A Karma that could, that would, cast itself over the lives of many others. A Karma that was more powerful than her own. And hers was astonishingly powerful. Grandma Djim sensed many parallels between herself and the young woman in front of her. But she knew that in her life of 80 years, she had never wielded the power that was now at Charli's disposal. Charli's aura was so strong and so clear to those who were not blind.

"We had a wonderful New Year's party. And then, three weeks later the Japanese came to my land, and everything changed."

Charli watched dispassionately as the old lady's eyes watered. The old lady, suddenly so frail, picked up her napkin and brushed away tears.

"I'm sorry… January 19th of 1942 is a day - a Monday - I can never forget. Ever. My life changed forever as Burma, my country, died."

The old lady let go of Charli's hands. Grandma Djim took her napkin and wiped away more tears from her eyes. She composed herself.

"I'm sorry, Charli. A lot's happened in my life but it hurts me always to remember the death of my country and the changes it caused me and my family. When my father was arrested, Jonathan, my husband, sent us to safety out of the city with a plan to catch up with us and get us all out of the country. I knew, soon, that the Japanese had executed my father. He'd been an important liaison to England and wouldn't tell them what they wanted to know about the English military strength in Burma and nearby India. I never found out what happened to Jonathan. I spent 20 years of my life trying to learn his fate before I reluctantly consigned him to the past."

"Less than a year later, I'd aged beyond my years. I was just 29. Not so very old. I'd gone from a life of high society to living on the streets of Rangoon. All the time, I had to hide our true identity from the Japanese. None of my former friends would help us. Married to an Englishman made us a danger. To feed my children, I sold my body on the streets of Rangoon to Japanese soldiers. I saved all I could so we could buy our way to freedom in Siam."

"Within a year of the fall of Rangoon, I'd saved enough to make our escape. Like others, we headed for the country, for the forest, trying desperately to get to Siam. I buried my eldest son soon after his fourth birthday. This was in forest south of Kawkareik. Unable to use major roads or the railway line, we were forced to travel by small roads, hiding out in small villages before having to move on. In the forest, we had no medicine to counter the malaria that had taken his body. As that terrible war ended, the remaining three of us reached the border that is the Three Pagoda Pass between Siam and Burma. My daughter was ill. I don't know what she had. But she kept on going because I'd promised her through our time in the forest that she'd see Siam. The Land of the Free. This was the dream she had in her brief life."

"She lived for two days in Siam and then she quietly slipped away in her sleep. I never knew what took her from me, nobody knew. In the night, I took her cold body back into the forest that had been her home. I gave her to the spirits of the forest, placing her where she belonged. She was very happy when she died, Charli. In death, I saw her smile as she'd never smiled before. Her face was lit with a radiance that had eluded her in life. She'd told me she'd spoken to her twin brother as he slid away and had promised him she would see Siam for him. She kept her promise to her twin brother. One day in Siam for him, one day in Siam for herself, and then she died. They'd always been inseparable. Twins are like that."

"I thought of crossing in to Burma to bury her in the same land as her brother. But then I realised only men make borders of land. God, if you believe in him, made the Earth. It was better that I placed her in the land that Man had chosen to call Siam. Twins buried separately in two countries that have long been at odds with each other."

"In the space of four years, I'd lost my father, my husband, and my two eldest children. All I had left was Yai. And he'd always been the sickly one. I knew for certain that he'd be the next to leave me. After the death of my daughter, my heart gave up living. For weeks, my mind was crazy. I remember nothing of this time, Charli. But I was told later that I wandered barefoot through the border camp and through the forest. I carried or, more usually, dragged Yai like some rag doll. I was ignored by others who had problems of their own to face. A few expressed pity for Yai, none expressed pity for me. Why should they?"

"There was no one to help me. I fought the dogs for scraps of food, and I still have the scars on my arms and legs from those savage fights. This was in spite of the fact that there was plenty of food in the camp. That's how crazy I'd become. I had nothing left to live for. Every community has to have the idiot - the one to be made fun of, laughed at. And I was the one. Nobody would interfere and I couldn't blame them. All had troubles of their own. If they'd known my true background, maybe they would've labelled me as a poor little rich girl throwing tantrums to seek attention. Finally, I cleared my mind and knew what it was I had to do."

"It was by chance we were found. I'd broken a bottle and had sliced Yai's wrists before doing the same to myself. Villagers found me clutching my dying son to myself in the rain and blood-soaked mud. It was only then that they made efforts to help us."

Grandma Djim showed Charli three deep scars on her forearm.

"That was my one crazy moment, Charli. But it worked. For weeks, I had been mad. And then I was freed, Yai was freed, freed from a living death, and I learned to live with my life. It was the richest lesson I've ever had, Charli, remember that."

I lingered with Yai for several weeks in the hospital. An Australian doctor who'd survived the Japanese death camps along the River Kwai ministered to us. He was a kind man but all I remember was his anger at my selfishness. Every day he told me I was a stupid, selfish, and thoughtless young woman. One day, Charli, I woke up and spoke sternly to myself. I put the past fully behind me. Exorcised it if you like.

"I find it ironic that of the three, it's Yai that has lived and thrived. I'm proud of all of my children Charli, very proud. Every one of my children helped me, at one time or another, to continue my life."

"I've promised myself that Jitta won't have to endure what I suffered and what each of my children suffered. I've made every possible plan for her future security. I hope I've left nothing out. So, if she appears to be smothered, please can you understand why this has been so? Yai has only the vaguest memories of his life in the forest. But he can remember the next five to ten years that it took us to bring our lives around. I'd had everything in Burma and was somebody. In Siam, I had nothing and I was nobody."

"At 32, alone in a new city like Bangkok, there was only one way I knew to make money to feed us. I sold my body, once again, as I'd done in Rangoon. Where before I'd gone with Japanese soldiers, now it was with allied soldiers. With the end of the war, there were many American soldiers in Bangkok. And they were lonely. To them, most in their early twenties, I was an old woman. But I had two pluses. I could speak good English where few of the Thai women could. And, being older, I was sexually experienced. Not like the younger ones."

"I don't think you could ever imagine what it's like for a mother to wake up and to realise that to feed her child, she must sell her body. You're so fortunate to have never had to make that dreadful decision."

Charli nodded. But said nothing at first. Finally, she spoke.

"You're right. Grandma Djim, I could never imagine how to go about making that particular decision."

"I hope Charli, and I pray, that you and Jay never have to face that. Belief, maybe not the right word, in my Karma was all I had."

"My life's been rich in many ways Charli. For a long time, I hated my past. But now I look forward to each day of the future. If I live only one more hour on this planet, then it'll have been good and it'll have been worth it."

She smiled through her tears at Charli who just stared straight into the old lady's face.

"Mai pen rai. That's not so important. But Charli. I know one thing about you. You think too much for one so young. Do not, as I did, think so much of your short past. It's not that important. If you do, you'll never escape it. It'll eat your soul and destroy you. And that'd be a tragic waste for this world. Think of the present. Think of the future. And like me, you'll then live to be old and to be happy. Have your one crazy act, like me, and then dismiss that part of your life. It'll be a rebirth. Trust me."

The old lady laughed. Charli looked up from the laughter and thought about what she had been saying.

The old lady got into the Mercedes Benz that pulled up outside the hotel. She wound down the window to speak with Charli one more time.

Charli remembered back to the moment when Lek's fingers had finally gone limp in her own hand. It was still just three months ago and the memory was fresh. She felt goose bumps as she listened to the old lady's words. She thought about the dinner date that she had agreed with Steven Hunt. As the black Mercedes pulled away, Charli tugged at a piece of loose skin at the edge of her thumbnail. The hotel service brought around her car. She tipped the doorman, got in the car, and headed off into the afternoon traffic. She knew now what she had to do.

CHAPTER 7

A change had come over Charli, a change that Hunt approved of. However, he was still confused about her. Her moods seemed to go up and down.

He watched her as she got up to go to the toilet. Relaxed from the alcohol, he leaned back and considered Charli. His initial impression had been that she was a lesbian. Especially when she took up with that Patpong bar girl. He was still unsure of her inclinations, but she had offered him enough this evening to make him believe there was some hope of thawing the 'Ice Maiden'. Charli clearly had something against men. However, Hunt had found her entire attitude strange - but at the same time attractive. After the disaster with Linda, he even wondered if his attraction was to stronger, more dominant women. And there was something alpha about Charli.

Hunt noticed that there was a definite femininity about Charli. She dressed spectacularly. He convinced himself that had she been nine or ten inches taller, she could have made a career as a model. Bill Rimmer had been right about that. But, there was a veil that shrouded Charli. Everything about her was seen through a soft focus. Interference prevented the picture from being sharp and clear. And he had learned that much of that interference was created, and controlled, by her.

But now? Recently with Charli there had been a definite softening of her 'Ice Maiden' persona. This night had proved it. She had even, after weeks of dodging, made a firm promise to take him to Khao Yai when he returned from the UK in April. And now that day had finally come. She had spoken so often about this forest. Hunt cared little for forests but he could tell that she was passionate about this one. For this reason alone, he wanted to see Khao Yai with her. If it meant that much to her, he would also make it mean a lot to him.

Hunt smiled as he considered this thought. And as he did so, Charli returned from the toilet.

"Something funny?" She enquired.

"Yes and no. It's not important. I was thinking that we've known each other, off and on now, for some two or three years. And I feel I know nothing about you Charli. You're an enigma to me. And do you know something? I like that. I didn't at first. I've never been one for surprises. But I'm enjoying slowly learning more about you each time. And I'm enjoying the surprises."

He linked his fingers together and rested his chin on the back of his manicured hands. He stared straight into her eyes. Lit by the candle, she was tonight, more than any other night, stunning.

Charli, knowing that she was fully in control, smiled at him and raised her wine glass.

"Good. That's just how I like to keep matters. But here's hoping you learn something more about me with each meeting. Maybe tomorrow you'll be lucky. Maybe tomorrow I'll let out all of my little secrets to you. Now. If you don't mind, I want to go to bed. We've an early start in the morning. You can stay until the sun rises and sleep in the car. It's me that's doing the driving."

Charli finished her wine. She wiped her mouth delicately on the napkin, which she folded neatly by her plate before she got up. She presented Hunt with a playful wai and thanked him, in Thai, for the meal. She smiled at him as she left. He knew now that he was getting close to the heart of Charli.

He watched her as she left the restaurant. He checked the bottle of wine and discovered that there was still a glass or two left. Before the waiter could reach him, he had poured himself another glass. The waiter stood by.

"I sorry, Sir."

The poor boy was embarrassed that he had been caught out not fully attending to his duties. In some restaurants and in some circumstances, Steven Hunt would have made an issue of this. But not here. And not now. He was too relaxed. He smiled at the still-embarrassed waiter. And spoke to him in Thai.

"Mai pen rai, krap."

The waiter thanked him in English and moved off. Hunt's thoughts drifted back to Charli. Back to the 'Ice Maiden'. Three years since their paths had crossed.

CHAPTER 8

It was at the trade fair that he had first seen her. He had just had one of his first business meetings with Leung Gait Fah. Mister Leung had insisted on presenting him with a small token of his appreciation for the business that they had concluded. They had finished a business lunch at an exclusive Chinese restaurant downtown.

Leung arrived with a young woman. She was tall and skinny. Maybe five foot six, but with tiny breasts pushing through the cheap dress. There was a wide spacing between her eyes, and her nose was flat, almost African. Her lips, however, were beautifully formed, and, like her other facial features, widely spaced. She was typically Isan-Thai. An original inhabitant of the land. Unlike Leung.

The woman sat through the meal and said nothing. Occasionally, Leung would put food on her plate and tell her she should eat. It was almost an order. When he did this, she made a gentle wai to him, which Hunt found endearing, and nibbled away at whatever morsels of food he presented her. It looked to Hunt as if Leung was feeding a pet dog. As Hunt watched, he could see that she was uncomfortable with the situation. He also guessed, correctly, that she was not happy with the Chinese food. She drank only water. As she drank, she kept her eyes down and held the glass with the fingers of both hands. He tried to work out how old she was. So difficult with the Thai.

At the end of the meal, Leung made a show of paying with his American Express card. Around his wrists were several large gold bracelets. Maybe a few thousand dollars' worth, including the gold chains around his neck, which held the obligatory Buddha amulets designed to protect him from all the world's evil. On his fingers were large rings with over-large gem stones. Jade, emerald, and ruby mostly. And Hunt knew that these were not fake. He guessed Leung was carrying at least sixty thousand dollars' worth of jewellery about him. It was all ostentatious. And yet it was small change for Leung.

They got up. The young woman rose silently and followed everybody from the restaurant and into the street. She kept her face down as she listened to the disparaging remarks of the Chinese elite.

"Steven, my old friend. I got many business to attend. You know me; always so busy. Like the bee make honey, take pollen from the flower. Have to flit here. Have to flit there. Flit flit everywhere. That's me. Just around the corner is my next meeting. I need fresh air to clear my head for this."

As he said this, a bus charged past them belching black smoke. Leung winked at Hunt. Leung grinned. Leung grinned with golden teeth all the time. But, especially when Leung grinned, Hunt was drawn to the diamond embedded in his first molar.

"Air in Bangkok number one, eh Steven? I walk. My driver, he take you go hotel. I know you've important seminar in afternoon. You need to be strong for your talk. For me, I've the important meeting with one staff who's not done his job the way he should. Aaargh. I've a good heart, Steven. You know me. But sometimes? Aaargh. Sometimes I have to be strict. I don't like to be, but I have to be. I think you understand me."

Leung addressed the woman. And, for Hunt's benefit, in English.

"Lek. You look after Mister Steven, okay? He very important for me."

He then spoke to her in rapid Thai. All the time, she kept her head down. Only nodding and repeating the polite word 'ka'. Finally, he gave her a business card. On the back, he wrote something. He grinned at Hunt. He belched and clutched his over enormous stomach before walking off.

As Leung walked off, Steven protested, but it was useless. The driver was holding open the door of the Mercedes for them both. Hunt and the woman travelled in silence for about 15 minutes. All the time, she sat staring out of the window clutching the card. Turning it over in her delicate fingers. She was picking at the corner of the business card with her nail which was coated in cracked, purple varnish. The nail, Hunt idly noted, was badly chewed. As were her other nails. When she was not picking at the card, she worked a small scab on her exposed thigh. This she did until a tiny spot of blood appeared. She wiped the blood away, leaving a smear across her thigh.

It had already dawned on Hunt what Leung's token of appreciation was. And he did not want her. And he was sure that she did not want him. Hunt had been coming to Thailand for a few years already. He had now taken up a routine where he spent three or four months a year in the country. Usually in two stretches a year. He had got an apartment. But for business reasons, and for this conference, there were many advantages to maintaining a hotel room. He was well known at this hotel. He knew, also, that this hotel would never allow a woman such as Lek through its doors.

He considered, briefly, trying to engage her in conversation. But as the journey carried on in silence, it became more difficult to break that silence. And she seemed content staring out of the window. Idly playing with the business card or the broken and now bloody scab on her thigh. He left Lek to her thoughts.

The Mercedes with its tinted windows pulled up to the entrance of the hotel. Hunt looked at the Thai, but she continued to stare out of the window. Her mind was elsewhere – a shaded pool, below a waterfall, deep in the forest. As the door was opened, he stepped out and continued to look at her. She did not follow him. But slowly she turned her head. She stared straight into his eyes. He was disturbed by the lack of expression on her face. Lek showed no hint of following him. The Mercedes pulled away.

Hunt passed into the lobby, collected his keys and three messages, and went up to his room. He began to idly scan the messages as the lift rose to his floor. Back in his room, he pulled off his tie. And then he laughed. He spoke out loud to the walls.

"Fucking hell, Steven, old mate. That was a close shave."

It was almost two in the afternoon. The afternoon session had already started when Hunt arrived. He went up to the meeting organiser and checked on his slides. The organiser asked him if he needed overheads. Hunt said no. Because of his association with Thailand, the local organisers had asked Hunt to present a main address. It was the one that would start off an after-tea discussion. He had wanted to get out of this, but could not do so. His supporters had reminded him that he knew so much about Asia and, more especially, about Asian business that it was important for him to present this address. Also, they reminded him it was important for him to be seen. Hunt had to present a higher profile now that he was becoming so important to Thai business affairs. Especially for the affairs of KA.

Hunt sat and listened through the last of the presentations before the afternoon tea break. A Russian warbled his way monotonously through a catalogue of New Russia actions. And then it was Hunt. Looking around, he saw that there were some seven hundred delegates.

Hunt sat back and felt confident about his presentation. The last three talks had presented slide upon slide of trade figures that nobody could possibly be bothered to take in. In 15 minutes, they could send the most problematic insomniac to sleep. Hunt had selected 60 slides to show, and he had 30 minutes in which to show them. And he knew people would listen. Because he intended to show holiday snaps.

During the break, with a cup of tea in hand, he drifted from one tea station to another. Getting himself refilled. He watched the animated groups discussing the meeting or arranging business get-togethers. And then one man approached him.

"Hello, Steve. Where have you been hiding?"

Hunt forced a smile. The Birmingham accent was one he hated.

"Sorry, Martin, important business. I even had to miss the morning sessions. I wanted to catch your presentation after you told me so much about it yesterday. Sorry about that. I was worried in case I didn't get back for my presentation. That wouldn't have gone down well with the organisers, would it?"

"Looking forward to that, Steve. I hope you'll keep us all awake. That bloody Russian had me doing me famous nodding dog impersonation."

Hunt's address was well received. And he basked in the praise. Afterwards, delegates looked him up. Business cards were exchanged. Pleasantries were passed. Eventually, he was able to excuse himself. Brummie Martin had approached him for a meal. Hunt had not wanted to be lumbered with the boring non-entity. He lied, convincingly, as he told Martin that he had an important date. that he could not put off. Hunt agreed to meet him later that evening.

CHAPTER 9

Hunt returned to his room. Opening the door, he had not expected to find her there. He had assumed that he had seen the last of the Thai in the limousine.

"Big boss-me say me look after you good. If not, me have problem too much. Okay?"

The business card Leung had given her was to get her through the back door of the hotel. Leung clearly had influence at this hotel which did not surprise Hunt. Leung had influence all over Bangkok. His business card was like American Express. Better. She was sitting on his bed watching the television and eating nuts from the minibar.

What happened consequently between them was clinical.

"How old are you really?"

"Oh really? I understand. Yes, me really, absolutely, genuine one hundred percent, cross my heart and hope to die, 18."

She told him that her breasts were also 18. Not like Katoey.

"For Katoey, body maybe 18, but breast maybe only two month. Not like me. Me not Katoey. Me one hundred percent lady."

She smiled impishly at him. He demanded to see her ID card to check her age. It came as little surprise that she was not 18. He was, however, surprised that she was 19. He guessed the card was a fake. It was, however, not. Lek had little idea of her true birthday. It had never been important.

She went to the bathroom. She locked the door. He heard her run the bath for a long time. He heard her bathe. While she did this, he took off his clothes. He pulled back the tightly covered sheets of the bed. He got under the covers and pulled one side free for her. He knew what to expect. He had done this before. Which was why he no longer went with these women. Masturbation was cheaper and just as exciting. The late afternoon light filtered through the curtains, although he knew it would be dark in less than an hour.

When she came out of the bathroom, she was wrapped tightly in the white hotel towel. She moved to the bed, sat down, turned away from him as she undid the towel, quickly got under the covers and turned off the remaining light.

After Hunt's moment of eastern ecstasy, Lek returned to the bathroom and took another shower. Martin Jacobs called Hunt and asked what time they were meeting for food. Hunt looked toward the bathroom and the girl and mouthed *fuck*. He had agreed to meet Jacobs but had no wish to take her with him.

As he got ready for the evening, he put the news on. Steven Hunt was only half-paying attention to the news when a report hit him like a bullet. The reporter's voice carried across the room, causing him to stop what he was doing and sit in front of the set. Lek was about to change the channel in her hunt for something Thai to watch. Hunt snatched the remote from her hand.

"Shock waves have been spreading throughout the City following the dramatic news that billionaire industrialist and philanthropist Sir Gordon Wessel was found dead on his estate this morning from a shotgun wound. The first reports have come from a leak which suggested he had died as the result of a hunting accident. Rumours, however, are now spreading, suggesting that Sir Gordon, 63, committed suicide. All attempts to contact his wife, Lady Elizabeth Wessel, have met with brusque refusals, which merely fuel speculation about his death. Given the renowned secrecy with which Wessel operated, this was no surprise."

Police have been at Wessel's Oxfordshire estate all morning. Sir

Gordon's secretary, Sarah Wilmington, was seen entering the estate some two hours after the discovery. It was, however, only at 10 a.m., some three hours after the discovery, that Sir Gordon's body was removed under a heavy police escort. We are now going live to Northrop Manor where Fiona Gray has the latest information."

The television cut to a scene of a reporter standing in front of an imposing set of gates, her hair being blown by the blustery March winds.

"It's now four hours since the discovery of the body by Sir Gordon's gamekeeper. A brief statement issued just an hour ago indicated that Sir Gordon left his house at about 6.20, supposedly to go rabbit shooting on his estate. His gamekeeper - William Saxby - heard a single shot at 6.40 and carried on with his duties. He became suspicious some 10 minutes later when he heard no other signs of activity and went to investigate. At just after seven, Mr. Saxby discovered the body of Sir Gordon slumped against a drystone wall. A single shotgun wound had blown away most of his face. The gun was lying by his right side..."

"Police are refusing to comment on speculation that this wound was self-inflicted. Questioning the staff shows that no note has yet been found to suggest that this is the case. There are no suggestions that Sir Gordon was suffering from financial difficulties. It is, in fact, rumoured that a major buyout of an American biotech company was to take place today. What will happen with that is unknown in the light of these developments."

"Sir Gordon controlled his empire with an almost patriarchal Victorian hand. Some City experts questioned his management methods saying these were more appropriate to the early periods of the industrial revolution than to the late twentieth century."

The report switched back to the BBC studio. A backdrop showed the smiling face of Sir Gordon Wessel between a dollar and a pound sign. A sombre-looking financial reporter spoke.

"The sudden death, this morning, of billionaire industrialist Sir Gordon Wessel led to panic selling once the markets opened, with some of the wildest trading seen since Black Monday. Already, city pundits are referring to the meltdown trading of the last few hours as Black Monday Two. Some stocks, notably those in industries owned by, or dependent upon Wessel, have seen massive losses. Petrochemical and pharmaceutical stocks, especially, are suffering with two to five percent average losses reported within the first hours of trading. In a separate report we'll try and analyse what this means."

"Rumours had been making the rounds over the last week that Wessel was about to buy the American biotechnology company GeneSys. Some had speculated that this buy out was to have taken place today. Our financial analyst Simon Speke has this."

"Coming so soon after Black Monday, the City is taking no chances. Fears that there could be hidden problems with Wessel Enterprises led to a mad, almost lemming-like rush to dump Wessel stock when the markets opened. Since the news broke, Wessel Enterprises has fallen five percent, reaching 2685 by 10 a.m. There are no signs of this dramatic fall stopping. We can only speculate, or standby and watch, how far Wessel may fall by the close of business, which is still the better part of a working day away. Experts fully expect a drop below 2000 and possibly as low as 1700, which could see almost a halving of Wessel within a single business day. City analysts are speculating that this could see the complete meltdown of what had, until recently, been considered a powerhouse of British industry.

One City contact I spoke to dismissed the possibility of such a collapse. Working for Barings Bank, he suggested such a collapse of Wessel would be comparable to Barings being wiped out overnight. In a word: impossible.

"Political commentators are noting that the PM has cancelled meetings for the day and has already started crisis talks with senior political, City, and banking advisers. The aim of this is to stop the possible wholesale slide in the Footsie Index which could develop if investors get worried about the knock-on effects that the collapse of the Wessel Empire could have on Britain as a whole. The Bank of England has said that it would not step in to bolster the pound and has announced, bravely say some, that market forces must be allowed to prevail."

Simon Speke was dramatically cut off as the cameras switched to Downing Street. A reporter stood in front of Number 10 as ministers were seen entering and other, anonymous, advisers left.

"The scene that you can see behind me speaks for itself. I've just learned that the PM has recalled the foreign and industry ministers from their trade mission to China. Already the Chinese are making diplomatic complaints over the 'loss of face'. But, at the end of the day, we have to ask: Whose face has really been lost? Ours or theirs?"

"Concorde, which was being used controversially for the visit to promote British technology, is expected to bring the two senior ministers back to London some time later today. We've been told to expect an announcement from the PM within the next hour. For now, it's back to the studio."

"Thank you, Charles. We'll return to Downing Street as we get further news of the government's plan of action. If, indeed, they have a plan."

Steven Hunt felt goose bumps rise over his body and mouthing the word *'Fuck'* he picked up the telephone and called London. With almost half a million pounds tied up in Wessel, he wanted out quickly and painlessly. He knew that this was a gut reaction, but it was one that he felt sure many other investors, large and small, were no doubt taking. It took several attempts to get through to Richard Graves. When he did, he got his secretary.

"Hello, Mister Hunt. Sorry you couldn't get us, but the phones are jammed following the Wessel thingie. And I should imagine that's what you're phoning about. To put your mind at rest, don't worry. Richard's taken care of everything. Ah, wait. Here's Richard now; he wants to speak with you personally."

"Hi Steven. I don't know what you've got out there in totty-land, but don't worry. I've everything under control. In fact, I'm rather proud of my little old self. You won't lose a penny. You're too valuable a friend and customer for me to screw up. This news has come as a massive surprise to us all. Absolutely massive, I can tell you. You couldn't even guess at the shockwaves it sent through the City. I saw four bodies fall past my window before it was time for morning coffee. God, there goes another one. Bye-bye Adrian. Never did like him all that much."

Steven Hunt interrupted Graves by screaming down the telephone. Lek, scared at this sudden flash of anger, sat nervously on the bed, not knowing what to do.

"Richard, I don't fucking care. I've the hotel news on here and they know diddly, pigging squat. We've got the BBC saying that Concorde is whisking the Foreign and Industry ministers back to London. They expect an announcement from the PM in an hour or so. Now to me, that is pretty fucking serious. So, stop joking around with me. I'm not amused. There's a rumour of suicide. That'd destroy Wessel, wouldn't it? I've never met Wessel, but suicide would surprise me very much. What've you got?"

Hunt stared at the phone and then looked at Lek perched nervously, trembling on the edge of his bed. He smiled at her. She nervously smiled back at him.

"We know about as much as anyone, but I've been working furiously on this. I promise. I've sent Flippa to prowl the streets to get what she can. She's fucking good, Steven - for a woman - and if there's anything, and I mean anything, then Flip'll sniff it out. A shotgun accident blowing your brains all over the quiet Oxfordshire countryside does, however, seem a bit suspicious, Steven. If you get my drift."

"Stranger things have happened, Richard."

"Be that as it may, Steven. It's still a touch rather curious. Flip's been getting rumbles through the jungle to suggest all was not well in the Wessel household. W.H. as you may surmise, is a far more important institution than W.E. She's heard a rumour that our Gordie was caught with a bit on the side and that darling wifey was none too pleased about this."

"But trust me, Steven. While everyone was dumping Wessel, I held on to your half mill because of some juicy little titbits from Flip. Just a few minutes ago, we started buying more for you. By then it was down to 2170. Believe me, you'll thank me. I've bought another 10,000 shares for you from the headless chickens. You're already up God knows what today. Obviously, you haven't heard the latest. Even I can't believe it. But the commission will allow me to get a down payment on a Porsche for George. The drama queen has been screaming at me to get him one for months now."

Steven Hunt had an eye on the television and could see that Lady Elizabeth and Sarah Wilmington had come out to make a statement. He had always trusted Richard's judgement. But from what he had seen on the news, he could not understand how he could be money up on events that had happened within the last few hours.

On a whim, he asked Richard the $64,000 question.

"The faithful secretary?"

"Could be, Steven. Could just well be. Who knows? And who the fuck cares? Lizzie and Sally did a wonderful duet together. Simply wonderful. That's what's getting everybody. The Wessel machinery was legendary for moving along silently, without so much as the proverbial gnat's fart. And even now in death, Gordie has the whole fucking shebang under control. Quite frightening, really. And it was for that, I held on to all your stock and then bought more. Wessel himself was powerful. Fucking powerful. But the reins have gone to wifey, and she's taken control without so much as a slip. The Wessel steamship never slowed an inch. It was awe-inspiring. Truly and utterly, fucking awe-inspiring, I can tell you."

"Lizzie made a prepared statement, which she insisted on reading from. It was terribly matter-of-fact. Not a tear nor a sob considering hubby's demise."

As Richard Graves told Steven Hunt this, he could watch it on the television in his hotel room. Hunt listened with one ear to his old schoolfriend while, with the other ear, he listened to what Lady Elizabeth Wessel was saying.

"Ladies and Gentlemen of the press. I apologise for the delay. I will issue this brief statement, and I then hope that you'll allow myself and my family some privacy at what is, for us all, a very sad time. I'll not answer any questions at this time, as I hope you'll respect the grief that we're all currently feeling."

"My husband, Gordon Wessel, was tragically killed this morning in a shooting accident. Ahead of an important meeting involving the four-billion-pound takeover of the American biotech company GeneSys. My husband got up at dawn to shoot rabbits on our estate. I'll add, this was a well-known habit of Gordon's. At approximately 6.45 a.m., while climbing a drystone wall, his gun accidentally discharged. Gordon suffered a single shotgun wound to the head. The wound, by its nature, was assumed to be immediately fatal."

"Our long-serving gamekeeper, Bill Saxby, discovered my husband at just after 7 a.m. I was alerted around 10 minutes later. I immediately alerted the authorities. Because of the effort, huge effort, that Gordon had put in to the takeover of GeneSys, I decided to continue as originally planned by Gordon. Hence the delay in this statement. I have, as you may all know, been involved with my husband's business affairs from a distance. And for this reason, I gave the authority to postpone announcement of this tragedy. In the meantime, the takeover went ahead, successfully, as scheduled, at 9.30 a.m."

There was a gasp of surprise from the assembled journalists. Those involved with business reporting carried on listening while also telephoning in the sensational news of the totally unexpected but successfully concluded takeover on their cellular telephones. This was the last thing that they had expected. It had been universally assumed that the GeneSys takeover could not possibly take place now. The Times financial reporter, who was monitoring Lady Elizabeth Wessel's words, was heard to exclaim that: *"I frankly do not believe a fucking word she's saying"*.

Lady Elizabeth continued.

"As an aside, I should say that this shows how close the links are between Wessel and GeneSys. Although delicate and drawn out over several months, we have always seen this takeover as a good one, a friendly one, for both sides. And, importantly, a good one for Britain. This acquisition of America's most innovative biotech company - at a time when trials of a novel anti-inflammatory drug are reaching a successful end - can only be of good to the UK and, ultimately, the world community. It is often forgotten that my background, before marrying Gordon, was in genetic engineering. I am therefore well-placed to both oversee and understand the importance of this acquisition."

"That's all that I wish to say now. I hope you'll allow my family the

privacy to mourn and to handle the funeral preparations of a great and a good man. A man who'll be sadly missed by myself, by our two daughters, and by the business world at large. Thank you."

Sir Gordon Wessel's secretary had stood silently next to Lady Elizabeth. Her expression was one of sadness. This was in notable contrast to the business-like approach of Sir Gordon's wife. Lady Elizabeth took the arm of the secretary and was about to go inside. A reporter shouted out above the other questions that were already being thrown at her and which she had ignored.

"Tell us, Lady Elizabeth, about Sir Gordon's alleged involvement with his secretary. Has that got anything to do with his suicide?"

Of the tens of questions that she was being bombarded with, this had all the ingredients to grab her attention and to demand a response. Sarah Wilmington burst into tears and tried to rush indoors. Lady Elizabeth grabbed the young woman's arm and almost violently spun her back from the door to face the tormentor. Taller than Sir Gordon's secretary by some five inches, she cradled the woman's head in her shoulder.

The assembled journalists and TV crews could see the secretary shaking as she sobbed on Lady Elizabeth's shoulder. Lady Elizabeth spoke into her ear, but her words were lost as she stared directly at the reporter. It was an image that would be carried around the world. Lady Elizabeth whispered into Sarah Wilmington's copper-dyed hair as she stroked her head. A few questions continued to be thrown at her, but she just continued to stare straight at the tabloid reporter. There was no emotion in her face as she watched his smirk turn slowly to a vacant look. The crowd was quiet as they watched the formidable Lady Elizabeth Wessel stare down the reporter. Over the shoulder of the sobbing secretary, she looked only at him. Everyone else ceased to exist.

Lady Elizabeth spoke.

"That's probably the most obnoxious question that anybody could possibly pose under these circumstances."

A few cameras clicked at the emotional sight that would be transmitted around the globe in a thousand newspapers the next day. Hunt sat transfixed, holding the telephone in his hand.

"I'll say this to you, Mr. Williams. I'll use all of my, not inconsiderable, influence to ensure that you never inflict such a question on another soul again. Your days in Fleet Street are numbered. Your employer is a close friend. Believe me. And as for your question. I shouldn't bother to answer it. But I'll say this."

Sarah has been secretary to my husband for three years now. But more importantly, she's a part of the family.

The very strength of Wessel Enterprise is that we all work together as a family. It's probably the biggest and most powerful family business in the world. As a family, we've a responsibility to ourselves, to our workforce, and to our shareholders. By becoming one of Britain's, if not the world's, most diverse and powerful institutions, we've shown that this method works. A method based upon respect that is mutual and a loyalty that is mutual.

"That a four-billion-pound takeover can successfully go ahead, on the say-so of myself and my husband's secretary, less than three hours after the death of the man who engineered it will surely attest to that. And believe me; Sarah's input to this takeover has been incalculable. That's why I called her around today. We, all of us, have a lot to do over the next few days, the next few weeks. I'll continue to play a powerful role in the company and, if invited to, I shall take my husband's position as I'm sure he'd have wished. And I can tell you this, Mr. Williams. Sarah remains a part of the company and, more and most importantly, a part of my family. She'll continue with us and will no doubt give me the same support that she gave my

husband. That is the Wessel way."

Steven Hunt watched as she kissed the secretary's forehead, turned her around, and guided her indoors. He was impressed.

"Thanks Richard. I've just caught Lady E's speech on the TV. Impressive. Fucking impressive. Do you think he was bonking his secretary?"

"It doesn't really matter whether he was or wasn't, Steven. Fact is, it's business as usual at Wessel. If Wessel had built the *Titanic,* she might well have still hit the iceberg, but she'd have carried right on sailing, leaving a billion ice cubes to melt in the North Atlantic. That was why I didn't sell your stock. And that's why I bought when I did. By the time of that statement, Wessel was down almost fifteen percent on the previous day's close. That was when I got you the extra 10. As of now, old chap, they're back beyond yesterday's close of 2973. 3071 and they're still climbing on news of the successful takeover. I've just netted you over 60k for a few hours' work. And I wouldn't be too surprised if they go above 33 by close."

Steven Hunt smiled to himself. He made a few rapid calculations and then spoke.

"Richard, there's about two million in number seven account that's doing nothing much at the moment. I trust you implicitly. If you think Wessel will go above 33, you've my permission to use that. Have you got me on that? You can spend that today. I'll call you at close of business and see how things went."

"Loud and fucking clear, Steven I'll be very happy playing with that."

After putting the telephone down, Hunt completed getting changed. He told Lek that he had a meeting and she had to stay in his room. He told her she could order whatever she wanted from the room service. Secretly she was happy with this arrangement.

He called to Jacobs and they arranged to take the lift together. The lift stopped at the ninth floor on its ways down. Hunt looked as he saw the copper-haired woman get into the lift. He had intended to eat with Martin in the Italian restaurant after first having a few drinks in the lobby bar. But when he saw that she had pressed for the lower lobby and the Thai restaurant, he rapidly changed their plan for the evening and decided to eat Thai. Martin raised no objections. He was one of life's followers.

That evening, despite the success Hunt had with the Wessel stocks, he considered the day a failure. He had planned to pass the Thai on to Brummie Martin and to bag the latest game for himself. But when she switched tables to sit with the Germans, he was left feeling like an idiot. He took the Thai girl for himself that night.

The next encounter with the quarry was also one that Hunt preferred to forget about. She had given him a very pointed brush off at the swimming pool the next day and it was about this time that Hunt had labelled her the 'Ice Maiden'. After drinking a beer and watching her from across the pool, he had returned to his room. In frustration, he had sex with the Thai girl. This also added to his frustration since she put no feeling into anything they did.

Hunt decided he would not be beaten. He had every intention of sleeping with the English woman tonight. He had learned from the desk that her name was Charlotte Harris. With new resolve, he decided to finally pass the Thai girl over to the Brummie and concentrate all his attention on Charlotte Harris.

Hunt successfully palmed Lek off and went in pursuit. He considered the evening a semi-success, although he did not end up with his prize. But he had made a breakthrough. He was genuinely horrified the next day to learn, from Charlotte Harris, what the Brummie had done to the Thai girl when she refused his demands for oral sex and his refusal to use a condom.

Lek had been expected to stay with Hunt – a gift from Leung while Hunt was in Bangkok. However, he quietly accepted matters when Charli Harris told him bluntly that she would look after the shattered girl. Lek refused all suggestions from Charli to take her to the hospital. It was then that the friendship developed. And for the next three years, Hunt found himself competing with the Isan woman for Charli's attention. Until she was finally removed from the equation.

CHAPTER 10

They left at 6 a.m. exactly, as Charli had told him they would. Hunt saw the car was loaded with her rucksack, walking boots, and a camera. There was also a picnic hamper and, he could not fail to see, an overnight case. Things were looking up.

Steven Hunt had always been direct in his advances. More often than not, this had earned him a slap in the face. But, more than a few times, it had got him a woman. After Linda, he had gone through a string of girlfriends. Most had been a one or, at best, a two-night stand. A few lasted longer. Hunt always believed that he tired of them and cast them aside. But if he was honest with himself – which he rarely was - he would have realised that it was they who invariably tired of him.

Linda had stayed with him for more than a year. By the end of their relationship, he had taken to unkindly calling her 'Lindy Homemaker'. Linda had wanted to get too involved with him. She had wanted to share too much of his life and to learn too much. She had done far too much snooping and this had become problematic. She had learned more about him than he had wanted her to know. Far more. In the end, he had no choice but to get rid of her.

But now, with Charli Harris, it was different. And Hunt had put this down to the awful start that they had got off to three years before, soon after the Wessel Affair. After three years, he still knew little about her but he accepted that. Finally, as he turned 40, he was ready for a drastic change in his life. He was getting older, and he wanted to slow the pace. Retire even, settle down even, have children even.

Hunt enjoyed the slow process of learning a little more of Charli each time they met. Knowingly or not, Charli gave away details over the years. A hint here or there over dinners together. He was a good listener. He gained small nuggets of information and slowly put these together to make a greater whole. He knew she was intelligent. She was well read but he didn't think she was well educated. Charli spoke little about her parents. All that he knew was that she did not see them much, if at all. Charli was independent. And given her intelligence, he assumed she had probably come up against her parents over education.

Hunt realised that Charli Harris was wealthy in her own right. He remembered back to their first meetings after the Wessel Affair. He had made a small killing with his shares thanks to Richard's sound judgement. Hunt was astounded by her knowledge of Wessel. Anything that he told her of Wessel came as no surprise. Charli had tried hard to give as little away as possible. But, thanks to the alcohol, she had made slips that he picked up on. She challenged errors and she often corrected him on small but subtle points. Often her information seemed to come from a source at which he could only guess. He challenged her at one point, asking if she was a Wessel employee. And that was where he believed he had finally caught Charli out. Her pause for thought was just a fraction of a second too long before she answered - no. She did, however, admit to having shares in the company.

As soon as they left the hotel, she put on music. Charli was talkative on the journey and pointed sights out to Hunt along the way. She asked him if he wanted to take pictures. He was surprised at her knowledge of the country and he told her this.

"All of this interests me, Steven. I like to see what makes a country tick. And this is it. I'm not talking about the hill tribe villages that the Khao San Road Brigade frequent. Hordes of budding National Geographic tourists following each other's bums through the denuded countryside, thinking that they're really experiencing the country. Stanley and fucking Livingstone. Burton and Speke. Clark and Lewis. Or was it Lewis and Clark? No, thank you. They're zoo visitors if only they had the intelligence to realise it. And I'm not talking about the Chinese businessmen that you deal with. The hill tribes are not Thai. The Bangkok city-tribe Chinese businessmen aren't Thai. What you see now, Steven, is the real Thailand."

They stopped at a small town along the way. At the market Charli bought food. Sausages on sticks. They were the only foreigners in the market. Hunt had never considered whether Charli could speak Thai before. But he was impressed with what Thai she could use in this small market. Charli told him that the sausages were made with pork and rice and stuffed into real pig gut. She noted that these were tastier than the Frankfurter-style plastic sausages that were popular in Bangkok. Sanitised sausages for the masses, she called them. Chicken breast was barbecued over a charcoal burner. Slightly blackened, Charli held it up for Steven.

"Gai yang aroy dee mak. Lek introduced me to this a few years back, Steven. She loved it. I used to watch her strip the chicken to the bone before tossing them to scabby dogs that clustered around the table. Usually there'd be nothing for them to pick. But occasionally she'd surprise me. She'd feed the best parts to the dogs and chew on the bones herself."

Hunt did not want to eat this food. Meticulous about hygiene, he had spent his life avoiding, as much as possible, the local food wherever he went. Thailand, Laos, Burma, or Colombia. Russia especially. But now, to please Charli, he ate the food proffered. He had to impress her. This day was a watershed in their relationship as far as he was concerned. Three years of working away at her and he did not want to upset the developments by refusing anything that she offered.

After Nakorn Nayok, they drove toward distant green hills. The car entered the park and began to climb through those hills. They had left the stifling pre-rain heat of the alluvial plains behind and, as so often before, Charli rolled down the windows, turned off the music, and let the sounds and smells of the forest float through the car. As they wound their way through the forest, she pointed out Heo

Narok Waterfall. Hell's Hole. She told Hunt of elephants that fell over the top of the 90-metre waterfall every few years. She told him it was also a dangerous place where several tourists had met their death.

"It's funny, Steven, how different cultures have similar names for things. Heo Narok waterfall's spectacular. Awesome. You should see it someday. Having said that, I'm sure you never will."

She glanced at him briefly and then turned her attention back to the road. Hunt looked at her. Puzzled at her certainty that he would not venture back to the waterfall. He vowed to himself that he would return and that he would bring Charli along as well.

"But I can see why it's called Hell's Hole. Like in Britain, there're waterfalls called Devil's Kitchen or Devil's Cauldron. I suppose they got the names because loved ones disappeared down them. Never to be seen again. Sad really. Because waterfalls are things of beauty. Power and beauty. Often deadly combinations. Don't you think Steven?"

Hunt answered yes. But this twist that Charli's conversation had taken was disturbing him. This was not the conversation he wanted for today.

The car continued to wind through the hills. Charli pulled off the road near some tattered wooden signs that had seen better days. She told him that this was a marked trail but followed on by saying that people rarely visited it. She told him that, on all her visits, she had never seen any sign of anybody going along this trail.

Charli then told Hunt they would leave the car and walk up the road. She told him there was another good trail through the forest. A trail made by elephants which led down to the river. She told him there was a small but beautiful waterfall where they could have lunch. Charli opened the back of the car and indicated the lunch hamper to

Hunt. She opened it with an exaggerated flourish. There was food, a bottle of wine, and cool beers.

Hunt could not fail to notice again that Charli also had an overnight case in the back of the car. He had thought of bringing spare clothes but that would have been too obvious. He agonised slightly because he never enjoyed staying in the same clothes for more than 12 hours. It was an obsession with him. His eyes were drawn to her overnight bag. Hunt picked up Charli's rucksack. He was about to shoulder this when Charli held out her hand for it.

"Hey, I'll take that. You're the male. You can lug the hamper."

Hunt did not complain. He enjoyed the fact that she had adopted the time-honoured role of the weaker female gatherer to his alpha male persona. Charli had spent three years testing him. Of this, he was now sure. She had played a primeval game in an age of otherwise easy sex. And for this, he now respected her even more.

They walked up the road. Charli led the way, Hunt followed, carrying the awkwardly-sized hamper. As they crossed a bridge, she stopped. She leaned over and stared at the boulder-strewn bed of a dried river. A few black pools of dead, stagnant water were all that was left. Although large, it was a seasonal river that was dry for almost three months of the year. The forest was nearing the end of the dry season.

Hunt moved close to Charli. She appeared, to him, to be in a secret world, and he had no wish to upset her reverie. He took out his camera and framed her face in profile with the dark, lush green of the forest as a background. His camera clicked. Charli turned instinctively at the sound to face him. In that instant, the camera clicked again. There was a momentary look of intense anger on her face. Hunt recoiled at the face that stared at him through the viewfinder. But Charli recovered immediately with a smile. While she was in this state, Hunt clicked more pictures. It all happened so quickly. For that one moment, when he saw her angered face in the viewfinder, he felt that he had destroyed all that he had worked so hard for. But when she smiled, he relaxed.

With each click of the camera, he studied her animated face and tried to guess what thoughts were swirling behind her green eyes. The early morning sun flashed off the copper of her hair, which he had never fully been aware of before. Looking at her face, Hunt realised he had never confronted such a mysterious, intelligent beauty in a woman so young. Or in any woman in fact. And it was this alien beauty that so much attracted him to her. And it was for this that he was prepared, for the first time in his life, to play by her rules and not by his.

They crossed the bridge and, a small distance further up the road, Charli showed where they could move in to the forest.

"So peaceful, Steven. We could be the only people left in the world. I love to listen to the sound of the forest. Far more beautiful than the sounds of the city. It's cleaner and purer here. Far less sordid. In everything."

Charli told him that the trail was used by a bird watching group, especially on weekends. She told him that this was how she had discovered the trail. But in the week? She assured Hunt that they had the place to themselves. A single word came to Hunt's mind as he remembered it was Wednesday.

Perfect.

Hunt continued to follow Charli through the forest. At first, he could see no trail. But as he adjusted to the conditions and looked behind and then in front, he realised there was a trail. There was the occasional burst of light where the sun blazed through the foliage and hit the undergrowth. In one such area, Hunt watched as a palm frond wavered lazily in a breeze that he could hardly sense. But such shards of light were few. It was cool in the forest, but also more humid. Rapidly, Hunt developed a sweat. His eyes stung as perspiration rolled down his face. He wished he had brought a handkerchief. Instead, he used the sleeve of his shirt. Anticipating the day ahead, he had taken extra special care of his appearance. It was, he thought, probably the first time that Armani had been worn in the forest of Khao Yai. But unlike Charli with her overnight case, these were the only clothes Hunt had. He grew uncomfortable at this thought.

They walked for half an hour before the forest floor sloped down to his right. Hunt had difficulty supporting himself as he carried the bulky hamper to the river. Charli walked ahead. A few times, Hunt had wondered if she knew where she was going. A few times, he thought to himself that he would not like to be lost in this forest. As beautiful as the forest was. And even if it was with Charli.

Charli stopped. She pointed out the blockage to their trail. A six-foot diameter spider web. Home to a black, red, and yellow spider with impossibly long legs. Hunt shuddered at the sight of the monster. He hated spiders.

At last, the trail stopped by the river. The lush forest suddenly gave way to a rocky valley of rounded boulders. The sound of a stream echoed amongst the stones. A stream, however, too small to account for the large rounded boulders of this river valley. To the left, Hunt could see water cascading over a small waterfall. It was not much of a waterfall and at first, he felt a sense of disappointment. But this disappointment disappeared as he knew that the place held enchantment for Charli. And that was important. She looked at him as he put down his burden. He let out an exaggerated breath and smiled at her hopefully.

Any boulder in mind, or shall we just do it here?

Charli stared back at him. Hunt let his smile fade.

"I thought you were tougher than that. All the squash you say you play? Soft city Boy."

He ignored her jibe.

"Charli? My god. How on earth did you stumble across this little patch of paradise?"

"Beautiful, isn't it? So peaceful. So quiet. I love it here, Steven."

Hunt carried over the hamper and placed it dutifully at Charli's feet. This was approaching idyllic. The two of them. Alone. Finally. After more than three years. He knew, now, exactly what was about to happen. He searched her face for some message, but he could sense no signals. Not yet. Later. She moved her eyes over to a flat area of rock. She flicked her head.

"Go, sun yourself. Take my rucksack - it makes a good pillow. I'll prepare things."

She threw the rucksack that she had been carrying through the forest over to him. He caught it and noted that it was soft apart from a bottle.

CHAPTER 11

The warm sun beat down on the exposed rocks and he lay back with his arms behind his head, savouring the moment. Hunt closed his eyes. He could see the red blood within his eyelids. He could hear the water cascade through the boulders of the streambed. He listened to the sound of birds calling to each other in the branches above. He listened to the drone of cicadas calling in the distant forest. Bliss. Pure bliss was all he thought about.

And Hunt could sense the soft movements of Charli close by. He opened one eye and grinned at her. She was standing over him. She stretched out her arms toward him. There was something strange about her behaviour that he had not encountered before. He looked at Charli quizzically. But then she spoke.

"Wine or beer?"

He uttered one word.

"You."

"That's not what I offered. Wine or beer?"

Charli held two bottles in her outstretched arms and offered them to Hunt. He pointed to the wine and then grabbed for her calf. Charli pulled quickly away from him and he slumped back. Content with the touch of his fingers against her ankle.

She wagged the wine bottle in his direction as if he had been a naughty schoolboy.

"Ah-ah-ah. Not so hasty, Steven."

The last sentence had been an admonition. But it held out some hope in Hunt's expectant mind. Charli took the beer and wine back to the hamper. She sat down some distance from him and opened the wine. She told him to bring over the food and paper cups, which she had left on some rocks in the shade.

They started on the food and they started on the wine.

"I still don't understand you, Charli."

Charli sniffed at him.

"What on earth do you mean, Steven?"

"Well, since I've known you, you've been involved with that bar girl. What was her name? Noi, Lek, Djim, Oi, Ay, Air, Bee, Beer, Bong, Nong, Mai?"

"Her name was Nongyao. Her nickname was Lek. It means small. Even though she was not small; she was taller than me. So, you assumed we were in a relationship?"

He looked at her sheepishly. Charli was chewing on a chicken leg.

"So, I assumed. I'm sorry. Look, I know she's dead now and I'm sorry. Really."

As Hunt said this, Charli looked at him. For the slightest of moments, she allowed herself a secret smile before carrying on.

How did you know she was dead? I never told you.

"She was dear to me, Steven. Very dear. I thought maybe I could help her. Make her life better. But I failed. She died on December 12th last year. I sat up all through the rest of that night and watched her ancestors come to take her away. It was icy cold that night, Steven. I sat in the park – St James's Park - and stared at the night. Christ, it was beautiful. I'll never forget the icy cold on my cheeks and my fingers. I had a bottle of vodka to keep me warm and I just watched a silent rain of shooting stars, which went on all through the night. Bright yellow they were. Beautiful. I'd never seen that before."

Hunt gave a little snort. He thought better of this though when he saw the way Charli looked at him. For the briefest of moments, he sensed a burning hatred. A forest bird squealed and her look passed. He had got used to her facial swings. And this was just another example.

"I'm sorry, Charli. I know you had noble intentions. Just like the countless fat and ageing farang men who take up with a Patpong go-go dancer. But she was just a prostitute. I'm not saying that it never works out. Sometimes it can. But 99 times out of a hundred. 999 times out of a thousand? Nope."

Hunt shook his head. He looked up at her and held out his cup for more wine. Charli stared at him. Hunt turned his gaze from her piercing green eyes. He had never been good with sympathy and condolences. Then Charli, almost dutifully, filled his cup.

"Thanks. Think, Charli, of how much money you spent on Lek. Think what you've got out of it personally. Don't get burned a second time. They're really not worth it. They're beyond hope. Sad, I know. But it's true. She's dead and you're still living. Live for today. It's beautiful. Live for yourself. You're beautiful."

He sipped his wine and lay back. Charli stared at him quizzically. There could have been a long silence. He felt awkward. But Charli changed the subject.

"This is not the best time to see this waterfall, Steven. Too dry. But then again, the rainy season isn't the best time either. Too much water. I like to come here in May and June. Or in October and November. It's beautiful then. There's a gentle cascade over the waterfall."

She pointed off to her left with her outstretched arm clutching the paper cup of wine.

"That pool has been sluiced out and is great for swimming in. The first time I saw it, I just stripped off and plunged in. Now it's too shallow. But in May? In June?"

She let the words hang. Hunt tried to imagine the waterfall and pool with more water in it and, most importantly, a naked Charli swimming about it. A naked Charli showering herself under the cascade of the waterfall. A naked Charli stretched out on these same rocks that he now stretched out on. Sunning herself dry. How many times had she done this he wondered?

But not now. There was an almost deathly stillness about the place. The birds and the cicadas had stopped their trilling. It was as if they were tuning in to Charli's words.

"It's a very romantic place, Charli. Almost like a secret garden of love. An Eden?"

She looked at him. He looked at her. One woman. One man. Eve and Adam. Alone in a secret garden. She poured him some more red wine. The drink of Dionysus. Hunt had now propped himself up on one elbow. She toasted him with her paper cup.

"You believe this is Eden? Plenty of trees. I'll give you that. But none of them are apple trees. There are a fair few snakes though. But you don't usually see many of them. And what good are they without the apple?"

At the mention of snakes, Hunt tensed.

"Can we change the subject Charli? I'm not so keen on snakes either. That's twice you've got me spooked. Once with spiders, now with snakes."

She laughed at him.

"Oh, Steven, you wimp. Don't worry. I've been coming to Khao Yai a lot and I can count on the fingers of one hand the number of snakes I've seen. Snakes aren't stupid, you know. They tend to keep out of our way."

She shrugged her shoulders at him. Hunt lay back and stared at the sky. He had been sweating in the heat and he felt his legs beginning to cramp. He began to feel uncomfortable. He needed water.

"Charli? Have we got any water?"

She told him to lie back and relax, and she would get the water. Charli got up from beside him. She ran her fingers down the inside of her thighs. She thrust her body out and then turned away from him. Charli moved away from Hunt toward the hamper, which she had placed sensibly, he thought, in the shade. She looked over her shoulder as he watched her rear encased in the tight designer jeans. Faded in two places around her well-formed buttocks.

He lay back on the rocks and closed his eyes so that he could concentrate on the tiny sounds of the forest. And of Charli moving about nearby. Hunt thought to himself.

Oh, fuck it. I am relaxed. I am having fun.

He looked at his watch. It was now one in the afternoon. In the dreamy past, he remembered Charli had said she should leave about four while it was still light. Three more hours. He looked over at Charli who was still in the shade of the tree.

Charli was 20 feet away from him. She turned, and in mock anger, she spoke.

"Oi! Stop peeking."

She turned her back to him. Hunt was unsure what she was doing, but idly hoped she was searching for condoms. He reminded himself that she had so far been prepared for everything on this trip. She turned and looked at him. He grinned childishly at her. This truly was approaching idyllic. The two of them. Alone in the forest. After three years. The warm sun beat down on the exposed rocks. He lay back with his arms behind his head. He rested his head carefully on a rounded boulder. Hunt closed his eyes. Through his eyes, he could again see the red blood in his eyelids. He could hear the waters cascade gently between the boulders of the streambed. He listened to the sound of birds which were again calling to each other in the branches up above. He listened to the returning trill of the cicadas calling all around. Rising and falling. And again, a strange-sounding solo bird that had caught his attention when it squealed earlier. He fantasised still further about a naked Charli. And he could sense the soft movements of her as she came toward him. He thought of opening one eye. But he decided to let the moment linger as he continued to watch her naked form in his mind's eye.

CHAPTER 12

Hunt's closed eyes, when they opened at the shock, were blinded by the sudden glare of the golden-yellow sun, set against the blue sky. It was the first time that he had stared into the heart of the boiling sun. He bolted upright as a thousand messages shot through his body and he looked maddeningly about him, thrashing from side to side. In quick succession, three more shots were fired. The second one hit the rock close by, showering him with flecks of lead and stone. The third bullet smashed into his left knee, while the last bullet also hit the rocks. The first bullet had grazed his right ear before ripping into his shoulder blade. But that third bullet had shattered his left kneecap. The damage, if allowed to heal, would leave him with a limp forever. Charli was, by now, standing a safe distance away. Her denim-clad legs apart, she cradled a nine-millimetre Beretta handgun.

As Hunt struggled to balance himself, he felt a pulse pounding in his head. It was joined by the pulse in his shattered leg and in his damaged shoulder. The adrenaline rush was causing all manner of messages to flash through his increasingly overloaded brain. All competing. And all competing with the unbearable pain that was telling him he no longer had a functioning knee. He was breathing hard and fast. Sucking the air into his lungs and gasping it out as soon as it had been depleted of usable oxygen.

"Oh Christ, no, not now, not here, not with you. Why?"

Charli had slumped down on the rocks some distance away. She cradled the gun in front of her. She levelled the gun and fired another shot. The bullet hit the rock some distance away, as she could now no longer look at him to aim. He screamed out a second time.

"For fuck's sake, Charli, what're you doing? Why?"

She screamed back at him.

"Why? You're supposed to be dead. It's not supposed to be like this. You're supposed to be dead."

Charli stood, levelled the gun and stared along its barrel. It was aimed carefully at his head, but she lowered the gun and turned away from him. She sat on a rounded boulder some way from him. Charli watched dispassionately. There was little need to worry about her safety now. He posed no threat and was not going anywhere quickly. And he was certainly not going anywhere without her help. His survival now depended on Charli.

But he was supposed to be dead.

Charli moved over to the shade of the riverside trees. She busied herself with the rucksack and occasionally looked back at Hunt as he lay in agony on the bare, sun-blasted rocks.

Again, he tried to speak. *Who sent you, Charli?*

"Who are you? Who the fuck sent you? Who paid you? I'll pay anything to stop you doing what they may have planned. Anything."

Charli sat looking at the gun.

You're supposed to be dead. It was supposed to be easy. Over and done with. Kim and Lek and countless others avenged. GD had told me to have my one moment of madness and then move on. This is it. You're supposed to be dead.

She wanted to scream out again at him that he was supposed to be dead. But she just looked up.

"What makes you think I had to be paid?"

"Why, Charli? Why? What the fuck's this for? What have I done to deserve this from you?"

Charli snorted at him. He lay on his right side, facing her. She moved away and opened a bottle of beer. She needed to think. This was not the plan and she had no idea what to do now. As Hunt lay on the hard rock staring at Charli, she drank the cool beer. The gun was resting on the rock beside her. He looked at it.

"You shouldn't have said that, Steven."

He tried to think what he might have said that he should not have said. What had he said to her that had caused this sudden act of violence? However, the gun told Hunt that there was nothing sudden about this. This had been planned, this was premeditated. And that truly scared him. More and more, Hunt was considering who may have put her up to this. A three-year contract? Hunt's mind was racing through half-thoughts and he could not think straight. But he knew he had to stop the bleeding soon, especially from his shoulder. While Charli's attention was elsewhere, he removed his shirt and pressed it against the wound, the sharp pain when he applied pressure almost causing him to pass out. Although his knee had suffered more serious damage, it wasn't bleeding as heavily. He hoped the pressure on the shoulder wound would stem the bleeding, at least for now.

"Said what? For Christ's sake."

"That she was just a prostitute. Lek!"

Hunt's mind raced again. He could not remember having said that. He had thought about it often. He knew it. And Charli must have known it. With every bar girl he had been with in the past, he had thought that.

No need to get attached to any of them. They're all just prostitutes. Fuck 'em, pay 'em and leave 'em. It's what they expect. All of them would go fishing with some hard-luck story hoping to catch a gullible farang. But I'm not gullible. They are there for a purpose. When needed, they are a source of sexual release. Not for any other purpose. Sexual release. No emotional attachment. A rubber doll with slightly more life.

But Hunt could not remember having said anything to Charli about Lek being just a prostitute.

Charli could see the confusion in his eyes.

"Several times, Steven. Just before, for instance. But one in particular. Last year, we were having one of our dinners. It was just before the Loy Krathong festival. You've probably forgotten it. Why not. It wasn't, she wasn't, important... to you anyway."

"The conversation came around to Lek. I'd said how I wanted her to join me but that she'd declined. She'd said she didn't like big hotels. She'd said she wasn't worried about the farang; she was worried about the hi-so Thais. The way they looked at her. The way they spoke about her and to her. The derogatory way that they called her, an Isan Thai, a Lao woman. Then you told me not to worry. She was just a prostitute, you said. It's what she expected, you said. Do you remember now? I'd said that it was so unfair. That a woman like Lek couldn't feel free walking into a hotel like ours. In her own bloody country. You'd told me that northern Thai are used to being called Lao. It's expected. You lectured me on the class barrier."

"But she was right, Steven. Do you know? I tried. Many times. I took Lek to many places. I helped her dress every which way. But wherever we went, whatever she wore, she was looked at that same way. If we spoke to anybody, they questioned her. Not me. Even apparently kindly people asked piercing questions of Lek. How did she meet me? Where was she educated? Those people have to know everything. Lek would say to me that she'd been grilled about everything. And why? Because she was Thai. With a farang. That's why."

"She wasn't part of the educated, elite community. She was Isan. And she looked it. She belonged in the maid's quarters. And they wanted to know what she was doing in their hotels."

Charli's anger at this injustice registered as she moved about, drinking from the bottle and gesticulating with it. Hunt lay on the rocks, half listening to her ranting and fighting against the throbbing pain from his knee and shoulder.

"If they'd seen Lek with a farang man, you can bet your life they would have dismissed her immediately as a bar girl. One hundred per cent for sure. When they saw her with me? They weren't so certain. But they still wanted to know what she was doing there. They wanted to know if she was their equal. Every fucking time."

"For some of them, they were uncomfortable in her presence. That was the funny part. A seemingly poor, uneducated woman could speak English. And many of them couldn't. So, they asked her what university she went to. What degree she had. And Lek was too ashamed to answer. Too ashamed to tell them that she had left school at fourteen."

"I didn't spend a fortune on her, Steven. I'm not stupid. Besides, Lek wouldn't let me. She was too proud. Although now I wish I'd been stupid and I wish she'd been less proud. I did help her get some nice clothes. I actually enjoyed dressing her. It was a challenge. But there was nothing she could wear that didn't cause the heads to turn."

Charli swung her arms wide.

"One time, I bought Lek some Calvin Klein jeans and a Boss t-shirt. The real stuff. Not fake. We went to the Nasa disco; Bangkok's biggest and brashest hangout for the rich, trendy young. When we left, Lek was in tears. I was angry at the way they had treated her. The way they'd spoken about her. Lek never wore those clothes again. I asked her what she'd done with them. She told me later she'd burned them and had then gone to the temple to say sorry.

Sorry because I'd made good merit for her and she'd destroyed the beautiful clothes. She told me that this was her Karma. To do only bad to those that try to do her good. Christ, Buddhism is a messed up bloody religion for women."

Hunt listened while concentrating on trying to make some of the pain go away. He still wondered what all of this had to do with him. He was even more convinced now that Charli had been sent by others to do this to him. It was the only explanation. He was even suspecting who might have been behind this. Leung?

When Charli stopped speaking, he listened to the silence that had fallen again over the forest. Hunt opened his eyes and he stared at her. His life was suddenly a million light years from his earlier expectations of this day. Surely this had not happened because of him pointing out to Charli what the girl really was. Just a prostitute.

Charli sat now, on a rock just ten feet from him. She held the neck of the beer bottle with the fingers of both hands. It hung between her parted thighs. In another age, this would have been an erotic picture for Hunt. As he looked at her, he noted she was wearing Calvin Klein jeans and a white Boss t-shirt. Briefly, he wondered, stupidly, if they were the dead girl's. But then he recalled she had burned them.

The blue sky above the river. The same bird with the distinctive call that he had heard earlier in the day was calling again in the trees. The chorus of cicadas had started once more. For what seemed, to Hunt, like a long time, Charli was silent. She had put the half-empty bottle of beer down and was digging at some dirt in a hole in the rock with a stick that she had found. Hunt was unsure what to say further to her. Still less what to do. All that he now knew was that this woman whom he had tracked for three or more years now had him trapped. He tried to remember how far he was from the road. But he gave up because of the futility. All that he could remember were the trees. Too many of them.

Hunt glanced to his right. Charli appeared alongside him. Standing above him, he could look up the length of her slightly parted legs. At the cleft in her tight jeans.

"Why Steven? Why should I help you? You're supposed to be dead. This isn't supposed to be happening. I'm supposed to be in a hotel now, calming down. That's what the overnight bag is for."

He shook his head. He thought. Thought for his life.

"For Christ's sake. Charli. We've known each other now for three years. Why this? And why now?"

Charli looked over her shoulder as she walked away from him.

"Yes, Steven. And in all that time it's not needed a very high IQ to realise that your interest in me was in what I have between my legs. Say it, Steven. Do you want me to undress for you? Show you everything? Say it. I'll do it. For me, it's easy."

Charli started to lift off her white t-shirt.

"Stop it Charli. That's not what I want."

"No? You don't want to see my tits?"

"No... not now."

Charli put the t-shirt back down. She looked at Hunt as he lay back on the rock. She snorted at him. And then she turned from him and continued to the shade.

You're supposed to be dead.

"Charli, I'm sorry for you. Just give me a fucking chance. Please. I want to help you. I love you, Charli. Don't you realise? You're the first bloody woman I've ever said that to. I've the money to help you. Even with this, with what you've done. I'll help you. I promise. Because I love you. For Christ's sake, stop this now. It's not too late. Don't let this madness go any further. Get me away from here and let me help you. This was an accident, that's all. A stupid bloody accident. We can cover this up. We were robbed and I was shot. You take me to hospital and I'll help you. For Christ's sake Charli, I love you. I really do."

The laughter hit him almost as hard as the bullets.

"Oh, Steven. How chivalrous, Sir Steven."

She gave a mock curtsey in his direction.

He started to speak again, but she stopped him.

"Shut up, Steven. Shut the fuck up. Yes, Steven, you're looking for a way out, aren't you? It's a basic animal instinct, I know. We all crap in our pants and throw up when truly fearful for our miserable lives. There was a time when I spent a lot of my thinking hours looking for a way out. But the way out never seemed to come. Not for Kim, not for Lek, not for me and now, not even for you."

Who the hell is Kim? And what do you mean about you and no way out?

"For fuck's sake, you deranged bitch. What… what have I done to deserve this from you? Why, for Christ's sake, are you doing this? Who, for Christ's sake, sent you? What, for Christ's sake, are you?"

Charli glared at him.

"We'll take that last question first. The what I am. Sorry, Steven, but I'm not prepared to tell you what, or who, I am. The first question; who sent me. It's more of a what sent me. Heroin, Steven. Heroin sent me."

"Oh, for Christ's sake, Charli. I know now. It's your friend. Noi."

"Lek, Steven. Her name was Lek."

He continued.

"The way she died with that heroin inside her. Believe me, Charli, I'm truly sorry. I know, now, how dear she was to you. I'm sorry. Truly. Look, there's a lot you and I can do to help people like her. Let me help. I love you, Charli. I truly do. Help me and I'll help you. I love you. Please help me."

"Steven, there's nothing you can now do to help Lek. You need to think of yourself. And how did you know what happened to her? How did you know how she died? I don't recall telling you. And I've a pretty good fucking memory."

He was caught off guard.

"I told you she'd died, and I told you when. But I don't ever recall telling you how she died in agony with heroin-laden condoms in her ruptured gut. I was there, Steven. I saw her die. In front of me. I held her hand, and I felt her skin go cold as she went from me."

"Have you ever seen somebody die? Have you ever felt somebody die? Have you ever been around when a friend, a loved one, has drifted away from you? Somebody who means something to you? Have you? Lek died in a room, in a hospital, far from where she lived. Can you imagine the horror, the loneliness, and the sheer torment in that moment, Steven?"

Hunt watched her face and looked at the eyes for some sign of compassion. But there was nothing.

"Lek told me she'd never taken heroin before. But it was always offered in the club where she worked. By her boss – your friend. Ironic isn't it? She died with almost a kilo of the stuff inside her. Can you imagine the agony? That's almost two or three per cent of her body weight."

Hunt had lain back on the rock again and was staring at the far too blue sky. He knew what agony was. He was suffering it right now. Suddenly things were fitting into some semblance of an understanding. And for this reason, he was becoming truly scared for his future.

A cool breeze ruffled the trees and he felt goose bumps. In the tropics? He spoke.

"Lek was a part of that life and I'm sorry you were involved in that because of her. Oh God. Looking back, maybe I was, partly, to blame. After all, you met her because of me. She was just some prostitute who'd been handed to me as a perk. Please understand me. I know what that Brummie shit did to her and how she looked to you for help. I wish, now, I'd done more."

Charli snorted again at him. He took notice. Her tone was mocking.

"There you go. Again, Steven, it's so easy."

"What do you mean?"

"Just a prostitute! You've known me for three years now, Steven. You've tried every trick in the book to get my knickers off and to climb inside me. But you know nothing. Absolutely nothing. My friend died in pain. Agonising pain before my eyes. These eyes, these sea-green fucking eyes, which you've lusted over in the belief they spoke volumes. Volumes of what?"

Again, with some gathered strength, he threw himself forward.

"I'm in pain, you deranged bitch. Because of you. Help me. Stop wallowing, Charli. I'm sorry you saw your friend die. But she was a prostitute, and she knew what she was letting herself into. Like all of them, she walked into the game with eyes and legs wide open. I'm suffering the same agony… pain. Worse pain. I didn't ask for this. And it's because of you. You fucking bitch. You aimed to kill me and failed. Do one of two things now Charli. Either get up the courage to finish what you started. Or get me out of here. You're not a sadist, I know that."

Charli walked away from him again. Back to the shade of the trees. This was not going according to plan. And he was right; she was not a sadist. He was supposed to be dead and everything was supposed to be finished. Not this. Plan A had been a dead Steven Hunt and his body rolled into a pothole in the river bed. There had been no Plan B. She now knew that she was incapable of pointing the gun at his head and finishing what she had started. As she sat staring at him, Plan B suddenly popped into her head.

She moved over to where he had neatly folded his jacket and went through the pockets. She took his keys, she took his pocket diary, and she took his wallet. She picked up his camera and studied it. She opened the back and she removed the film. Exposing all the pictures that he had taken of her earlier in the day. Which seemed an eternity ago.

"Thank you, Steven."

She moved back to her place in the shade and placed the articles in a pile beside her.

"Have you ever been to one of those girlie bars, Steven, in Bangkok? Of course, you have. Don't answer. Stupid question."

As she was speaking, Charli idly picked through the items she had taken from his pockets. She noticed a new, unopened packet of condoms, which she held up.

"How thoughtful. I wonder who you had in mind for these."

Charli turned her attention to his wallet and picked through this, examining his credit cards and the business cards which he had collected along the way.

"You said she was just a prostitute. Have you ever thought, Steven, what those girls are thinking when they're dancing for you? Have you, Steven? In any of those bars, there are girls who are so stupid that if you took them away and gave them a million pounds, they'd lose it all gambling and be back the next day. There are also girls who are so bright but who have had no opportunity so that they're now imprisoned. Always looking for a way out. Hoping for the man of their dreams. It rarely happens. Knights in shiny armour are so very few and so very far apart these days. They all got eaten up by dragons, I guess. But in the middle? The other ninety per cent? You're quite clever. You should think, Steven."

His voice whimpered.

"I'm sorry."

Charli spoke as she continued to idly look through his diary.

"I thought I was getting out of a deep, dark hole until I met you. Things were beginning to go right for me for once in my own miserable, bloody life. And then you came along. To screw everything up for me. Well, I'm sorry. I'll not let you screw up my life now I've come this far. Or anybody else's for that matter. I've become too strong now. For once, I'm in control. And do you know something? It's a good feeling to be in control. It's a very fucking satisfying feeling. And I could get used to it. I am getting used to it."

A coldness came over Hunt at these words. He knew what she had said but did not believe, at first, what he had heard.

"You've always wanted sex with me, Steven. Haven't you?"

Hunt turned to look at her. She was sitting with her arms wrapped around her legs. Her chin rested on her knees as she stared at him. She smiled. Another beautiful photograph.

"Don't deny it, Steven. I'm not stupid. Who the fuck, just for example, were those for?"

She threw the condoms at him. He whimpered under his breath.

"I never considered you stupid, Charli."

"I'm a woman Steven. Your kind consider all women stupid. Ever since you first clapped your eyes on me, you've slavered over my body. Admit it, Steven. I can still remember the way you tossed aside Lek in the hope you could chase after me. She'd been given to you by your business friend on a plate. I know. Lek told me. But you thought you could go for me. That's true. Isn't it, Steven?"

"No, it isn't. I didn't."

Hunt was lost for words, knowing the position he was in and the feelings his captor had for the dead prostitute. He lay back, trying to compose a reply. Charli answered for him.

"Bloody hell, Steven. Admit it. She was just a prostitute. Handed to you on a plate and you didn't want a freebie. I don't know. Maybe you'd read the local paper that day. Can you remember the front-page news? I can. It said a recent government/WHO study had shown that an HIV explosion was about to hit Thailand. Still hasn't, mind you. It gave statistics on prostitution and it made, for me, frightening reading. Maybe having read that, you thought you'd better play safe and chase some cleaner pussy. Is that what you thought, Steven?"

"Maybe yes, Charli. If that's what you want to believe. Yes, I'm sorry. That was at the back of my mind. HIV. But I hadn't read the paper. I was angry this girl had been given to me in such an off-hand manner. I was insulted. And I'm sorry. Truly sorry if you now feel offended that I only directed my attention at you as a way to get rid of her. I'm sorry. That's not the way it was. Believe me. You should look in the mirror and realise the power you have. If I'd really been like that, do you think I'd have pursued you as doggedly as I did for three years? No."

Charli snorted in disgust and moved away.

"Do you know anything about Patpong bar girls, Steven?"

Hunt closed his eyes and nodded no. It seemed the safest answer.

"I thought not. There are some girls who try to get bought out every night. But not many. They get paid a flat rate for dancing. Did you know that? They get paid some more if they take their tops off. More again if they go nude. They get paid a bit more if they supply a speciality act. You know the kind. Using chopsticks, opening bottles, writing, smoking, that kind of thing. Good for a giggle, eh Steven? Admit it. I bet you've had fun watching some of those shows."

He recalled some of the shows that he had taken visitors to. Everyone enjoyed the titillation.

"When you were offered Lek, they offered you one of the newest girls. Don't worry. She wasn't a virgin. She was eighteen - or thereabouts. Maybe nineteen. She'd worked at the club for a few weeks and she told me she'd been with seven men. Whenever she went out with a man, she had no idea really where it would lead. One time she got beaten up."

Charli shrugged.

"Hazards of the game, I suppose, Steven. A bit like your work. That must involve risks. But you put up with it, don't you, because of the big rewards. You could view your current predicament as an occupational hazard. The same as Lek."

And you say you were worried about catching HIV from her. I don't know, Steven. But I think you missed a relatively safe opportunity. She'd probably had less sex and with less men than any of those air hostesses that swan around the swimming pool back at the hotel. You know the ones I mean.

Instead, you ended up with me."

Charli laughed.

"That was a tough one. Maybe you should have stuck with her. With Lek. She'd probably have been a lot less harmful to your health than I am."

Her words drifted over to him. Hunt turned his head to her. He was still looking for a way out. Any way out. There had to be. She was crazy. There was no doubt about that now in his mind. But she was also very clever, and he was still sure, working for others. But again, he refused to believe that there was no hope for him to get out of this predicament. All he had to do was get back to the road. They had walked the distance in thirty minutes or so. He felt sure that even in his current state, he could crawl back in a few hours.

"Lek, as you said, had just started. But what would she have been like after a year? After two years? Three years? Okay. When she was handed to me, she'd been with a few men. Or so she said. If she kept to that? After three years, how many? I don't know what the real fucking statistics are. Who does? Let's say after a year she'd become immune to it all and was averaging ten a month. Over three years, that's over three hundred men. Maybe some would have been the same ones. But even so, Charli. Even so. How long do you think it would have taken before something gave? In body? In mind? In health? Whatever?"

And tell me, Charli. If you've been to the clubs, like I have, tell me; how many girls have you seen strung out on pills. One thing, for them, leads rapidly to another. How long before they're on the hard stuff. The heroin and needles. That's when they're most likely to get HIV. I'm sorry Charli. I didn't want to take the..."

"Shut up, you fucking sanctimonious bastard."

Her speed shocked him. Hunt struggled to move but he was not quick enough and didn't have the strength to move far. She moved rapidly over to him and stood, pointing the gun at his head. He squinted at the sun that was behind her. He held his hands in front of his face. For all that was worth. The bullet would merely shatter a few more bones before destroying his head. He screamed at her and the forest birds went silent.

"Do it, you crazy cunt. Go on, pull the trigger. But before you do, for Christ's sake tell me who sent you and who paid you to do this. I have to know."

"Move, Steven. Over there. To the river. Now."

He began to drag himself along the ground. His mind was racing as his hopes of escape, of freedom, or even of overpowering this woman appeared to be disappearing. Charli followed him. When he was close to the middle of the stream-bed, he looked at her pleading.

"Where now, Charli?"

"Over here Steven. Over this way."

She pointed to her feet. He crawled toward her. He could see she was standing next to a hole in the dried stream-bed.

"Get in, Steven."

He shook his head and moaned.

"No, Charli. No, don't do this. Please."

She pushed him toward the hole and he struggled to stop himself from falling in. But he had no strength to resist.

He dropped to the bottom and screamed out as he landed on top of three rounded stones. There was a small pool of blackened, foetid water around the boulders. He looked up at the sky at the top of the hole some seven feet above his head.

"It's not deep Steven. Only about six, maybe seven feet. If you stood up you'd be able to reach out and pull yourself out."

"You fucking mad crazy bitch. I can't stand up."

"Such language. Yes, Steven. I am crazy. I'm also dangerous to your health. Lek never was. That's my point. She was your victim."

Her silhouetted, once beautiful, face looked over the edge of the hole.

"It's getting late. You need to rest and I've a long drive back to Bangkok."

After all that had happened, an even colder dread came over Hunt as he heard these last four words. Charli leaned over the hole and looked at him.

"What's the best way back to your place? Do I just go down the highway and pull off onto Sukhumvit? Or is it better to work my way around the back streets?"

"What the fuck do you mean?"

"I'm going to visit your apartment, Steven. There are a few things I want to check out."

He snorted briefly.

"You'll never get in Charli. There's security on the building and Djoi, my maid, lives there all the time. Give it up, Charli. Whatever it is you're looking for. Give it up. You won't find anything. Get me out of this hole, get me to a hospital, and I'll help you with whatever you want. Whoever is paying you to do this, tell me. I'll pay you more to stop it. I've got the resources. You must know that."

"Thanks for telling me the maid's name is Djoi. That'll be useful."

As Hunt stared at her face, she smiled. The smile that had appeared in the viewfinder of his camera was the same smile. The eyes were the same eyes. But the face was filled with menace. And then Charli was gone. He waited a moment before he screamed out her name. He listened, but there was nothing. He screamed out her name once more, but she did not return.

Hunt leaned back against the wall of his prison There was an annoying pulse in his shattered ear. He raised his hand carefully to test the damage. As he probed the side of his head, Hunt was aware that his ear was still in place. But it was damaged. Apart from the pulse, there was a high-pitched whine that drowned out any other of the far-off sounds of the forest. Although his outer ear could heal, his inner ear was so badly damaged that he would likely never hear with it again.

He looked about his prison in the late afternoon gloom. Apart from the small pool of stagnant water, the pothole was very dry. The walls were encrusted with a blackish green alga that had formed as a film over the rock as the hole dried out.

"You fucking crazy bitch. Who sent you?"

CHAPTER 13

Charli worked her way through the forest as she headed back to her car. When she reached the road, Charli was careful to check for passing traffic. The sight of a farang woman stepping out of this remote part of the forest would be remembered if Hunt was ever found. She stopped at the bridge to look up the river. She held the camera that he had used and smashed it on the concrete of the bridge before brushing the broken pieces into the river bed. She watched as three of the larger pieces scattered amongst the boulders below. The film that she had removed earlier, she hurled farther up the river. For a brief while, she could see the black ribbon trail behind the yellow canister. When it came to rest, it was hidden from view.

When she got back into the car, she sat for several minutes. Her heart was racing and she could sense a migraine coming on. She looked at her watch; it was gone three in the afternoon. Charli set off driving as fast as she felt was safe through the winding grey ribbon of tarmac that snaked through the forest. She was heading south along the same route that they had taken when they left Bangkok.

She knew she had to travel fast to cover the 170 kilometres. Leaving the park behind her, Charli drove hard back to Bangkok. For the first 70 kilometres, there were few problems. She could pass the lorries, most cars as well. At one point, a pickup truck tried to race her. Charli had to spar with this for 10 kilometres. Especially after the teenage driver and his four friends had noted that they were racing not just a farang but a woman as well. A boost therefore not only for their country but also for their manhood to outrace her. Her car could accelerate faster than the diesel pickup but when Charli was stuck behind a lorry, waiting for a safe opportunity to overtake, the pickup would charge recklessly past her and the lorry. The young driver cared little for his safety or for the safety of other road users. If he had an accident, that was his Karma. Sometimes, he overtook on approaching bends. Sometimes on blind bridges that crossed the many canals which fed the rice fields. However, often the driver of the pickup truck would just undertake on the dirt shoulder by the side of the road. Eventually Charli was able to leave the pickup truck blocked and unable to undertake. Slowly, she put more lorries between her and the pickup. She did not see it again.

The rest of the journey was uneventful and she arrived at the hotel just after 6 p.m.

Once in her room, Charli showered and changed. At 7.15, she walked a couple of streets from the hotel, hailed a taxi, and headed for Hunt's apartment. When Charli dismissed the taxi a few hundred metres from the lane where his apartment was located, she watched it head off before she started walking. Two old ladies, bent double with age, picked their way slowly past some drains which were about to be lined into the hole that ran the length of the road. They used the large pre-cast concrete pipes for support. They clearly did not have the cushion of wealth that Grandma Djim now enjoyed. Charli stepped into the road to get around them. As she passed them, one woman looked at her. It was impossible to feel what the woman was thinking, so Charli avoided her eyes and walked quickly by.

Hunt's apartment was down a small, poorly-lit lane. It was close to what passed for the Arab quarter of Bangkok and was surrounded by many northern Indian or Pakistani restaurants. Several boasting Halal cuisine for the many Saudi businessmen who stayed in the area. She reached the address of his condominium.

There was a reception desk with two men behind it. Nobody looked up at her. To the left were three lifts. One had its door open. A uniformed guard sat looking at Charli with a bored look on his face but he did not question her. He recognised Charli as a farang. His job was to question suspicious-looking characters, especially Isan-Thai such as himself. Obvious low-class trouble-makers or potential thieves. Or prostitutes who had not been invited or who had not checked in first. The guard concluded there was nothing suspicious about this woman getting into the lift. She was clearly not Isan; she was dressed with money and he did not want the trouble of trying to communicate with her. He spoke no English. Charli smiled at him as she pushed the 'close' button. He stared back. For a farang, she was small and pretty, he thought. Most of them were big, fat, and ugly.

Inside the lift, Charli pushed the button for the tenth floor. There were three apartments numbered 101, 102, and 103. Charli stopped outside the reddish-brown heavy wooden door of apartment 102. She adjusted her clothes and checked her appearance in a mirror. She rang the bell. After a short while, she was aware of somebody scrutinising her from behind the door. As the door was opened gingerly, Charli stepped confidently into the small vestibule, giving the surprised maid no chance to react.

"Hello, Djoi. I've come to see Steven."

Before the maid could stop her, Charli had moved further into the apartment. Djoi left the door opened but turned around.

"Khun Satee-wen is not here now. I not see him since yesterday already. He go away Krungthep."

As an afterthought, the maid continued, not knowing who Charli was.

"He tell to me his girlfriend - Charli - take him see forest Khao Yai."

Charli was slightly startled at this, but did not show it. She turned and smiled at the maid.

"That's okay Djoi. He'll be back in about an hour or so. I spoke with him after he left... erm Charli, and he told me to come round first and make myself at home. I've some wine I want to cool. Steven said I should give you 4000 Baht to go out with your friends some place."

The maid's face dropped at this. Hunt had usually given her 200 Baht, which was more than enough. But 4000? That was almost a month's wages for her. Khun Steven had sometimes got her to leave for the night when he wanted to entertain a girlfriend. The maid knew he had many girlfriends. But those women were always Thai. And Djoi suspected that most of them came from Patpong or the nearby Nana Entertainment Plaza. She could tell from the way they spoke and the way they dressed. She did not approve of this. But so long as he had sex with these girls and not with her, all was fine.

"4000 Baht? Khun Satee-wen only ever give me 200 before."

Charli smiled.

"Yeah, that's what he wanted me to give you. Tight-fisted sod, isn't he? The rest is from me. Okay? That's my thank you for you leaving. Go out some place, Djoi. Enjoy yourself. I'll look after Mister Steven very well tonight. Come back about 10 tomorrow morning. Take an overnight bag. I'm sure you've some friends you can stay with. If you show me where the kitchen is, I'll look after myself and Steven."

The maid took Charli into the kitchen and showed her around it. Her small bedroom was off the kitchen. Charli fixed herself a glass of wine and moved back into the lounge. She sat on the sofa, nursing her drink and waiting for the maid to reappear.

Presently, Djoi came out of her room. She had changed and had a small tartan shoulder bag with a white cuddly bear attached to it. She smiled at Charli. Charli was briefly taken aback. Isan, like Lek, she had the same wide and bright smile. Charli found her very pretty. She carried some books. "English for Beginners", "Hotel Accounting" and "Customer Relations".

"Are you studying?"

"I 19 only now. Family of me give money study at Ramkhamkaeng University. In future, I will work for the big hotel and have good job. This I know."

The Isan girl's confidence touched Charli. She had assumed that she might have been a pick-up from Patpong. But she believed her in this.

"Off you go, Djoi. I'll look after Mister Steven tonight. Okay? And when you see him, you should get him to raise the two hundred to five hundred Baht. I can see you've a lot of books to read for those courses."

The Isan girl covered her mouth with her hand as she giggled and left the apartment.

Djoi stood by the lift, trying to decide what to do. She had a few friends, also maids, in the apartment block. But apart from this small community, she knew nothing of Bangkok. She sometimes went to discotheques with the other maids. But these were expensive. Especially when the maids wanted to drink Johnnie Walker. Most of them had little education and only liked to drink, smoke, and gamble. Djoi drank whisky and smoked the occasional cigarette when out with friends. But she always resisted the temptation to gamble except for her weekly lottery ticket.

As always, when Khun Steven asked her to leave, she would go a few blocks away. There was a noodle shop run by a kind Chinese family. They always welcomed Djoi whenever she turned up. She treated this as her second home and her second family. They let her have a table in the corner to herself. She would eat some noodles, have water or, occasionally, a cherry Fanta. The owner called her his daughter and often gave her the Fanta for free. He and his wife had no children.

When the owner knew that Djoi was planning to work in a hotel, he taught her how to use an abacus. He also let her help out with his small noodle shop so that she would get practice at customer relations. Djoi helped him with his accounts in return for food. The owner had some friends in the small hotel trade and told Djoi that when the time was right, he would do what he could to help her. Although grateful for his help and kindness, Djoi had her sights set on the bigger luxury hotels of Bangkok.

From the 200 Baht that Hunt usually gave her, Djoi would come away from the evening having spent about 30 Baht. She would read her books until the light got so bad that she drifted off to sleep at the table. The noodle shop was open all night. About two or three in the morning, Khun Choong's noodle shop would get busy again as the tables filled with chattering girls of Djoi's age. Always laughing and telling each other coarse jokes. Djoi would sit and listen to their bawdy language. She did not like it. Sometimes a bar girl would bring her farang catch in. Djoi always noted that the girl would eat noodles while the embarrassed farang would sit and drink a beer, always looking nervously about.

Khun Choong told Djoi that these girls were not good. He wanted to know why all Isan girls could not be like Djoi. Polite, well-mannered, and not promiscuous to the point where they would sell their bodies to live. Djoi had no answer. But she asked herself the same question. She was hoping one day that she could get a good job at a good hotel. One that paid more than the maid's job she had now. The farang lady had just given her 4000 Baht. And this would go into her savings account. Djoi lived simply. Every month she sent 1000 Baht back to her family. And every month she saved one or two thousand Baht. After two years in Bangkok, she had almost 30,000 Baht saved up. She often wondered how much the girls who came into Khun Choong's had saved.

Chapter 14

Charli waited for 10 minutes in case the maid reappeared. While she waited, she put on a pair of cotton gloves and moved around the lounge with her drink in her hand. Near the television and video was a unit with an extensive array of books. There were well-thumbed tourist guides for Thailand, Malaysia, Indonesia, Burma, Laos, Vietnam, Colombia, and Russia. Next to these were road maps for Thailand, Malaysia, and Colombia. There were several paperback novels too; Tom Clancy, Michael Crichton, and some John le Carré. There were history books on the region, Thailand especially. Some books on the American involvement in Vietnam and Cambodia and a few books on the American CIA operations in Laos. The Secret War.

Charli continued her tour around the lounge. Hunt was a collector of quality *objets d'art*. From Thailand, from Burma, from Cambodia, and from Colombia. Colombian rugs and Burmese tapestries hung from the walls. There was Thai lacquer ware, some Khon masks, as well as Celadon and Niello. These were old. Not copies made for tourists and bought from the Chiang Mai night bazaar. There were stone carvings of Khmer origin, likely looted, and a variety of Buddha images. Steven Hunt had taste and Charli admired the apartment. In much of its style, it was not unlike her own place in London. Everything was expensive.

Charli moved from the lounge to a darkened hall. She turned on the light and was faced with five doors. One of these was open and was obviously a bathroom. She opened the nearest door and turned on the light. It was a bedroom with no character. There were a few pictures on the wall and a made-up bed. Charli opened the wardrobes. They were empty, with only a few hangers in them. There was a door that led to an en-suite bathroom. She turned off the light and closed what was obviously a guest bedroom.

The second bedroom was lived in. This was obviously his. The bathroom had a masculine feel to it. There were many expensive oils, soaps, and shampoos, all neatly arranged by the maid. Charli turned off the light and left this room, which smelled too much of Hunt. The third door was locked. From her shoulder bag, she took Hunt's keys and tried each of the likely ones in turn.

Finally, the lock clicked. She turned on the light, moved over to the windows, and pulled the curtains closed. She had thought of using a torch but considered this more suspicious. The Watergate break-in gang may have got away with their act if they had simply turned the light on. From outside, it was unlikely anyone would notice the light on in this room. They would, however, notice the beam of a torch in the darkness.

This room was originally a small bedroom, but the bed had been removed. In its place was a large teak desk and on top of this was a computer. There was a current diary and shelves of magazines. Along one wall was a stand of four filing cabinets. These were locked. Again, Charli could open them with the keys.

She moved back to the desk and turned on the computer. It ran through its start-up tests and then it stopped, prompting her for a password to get past the BIOS start-up.

"Shit."

Charli decided to leave this until later. It was possible she may find enough without having to look at his computer files. Another wall had bookshelves, and on one shelf was a stack of diaries. Charli skimmed rapidly through these and a picture began to emerge. She picked up the diary for last year and turned to the dates immediately before Lek had gone to Britain. As she found what she wanted, a lump came to her throat. She put the book down and went back to the kitchen. She took the bottle of wine from the fridge and went back to the study. She leafed through the entries.

There were cryptic messages about deals and arrangements. These could have been for anything, but Charli was now beginning to understand. Choo had to go to Khlong Toey to arrange the main shipment. There was a note that showed it had to arrive in Southampton on December 11. This date leapt out of the page at Charli. 'Must arrive' had been underlined heavily twice. The next entries hit Charli hard and left her gasping in anger.

As Charli barely contained her anger, veins stood out in her neck. Her hands shook as she held the diary. In some of the other diaries, Charli noticed similar references to mules who would be sacrificed to the authorities. Sometimes two girls were involved. One time, three.

She checked his filing cabinets. Under a section labelled 'EMBASSY' Charli found many letters. These were all listed from bogus companies. There were three for Lek. These letters were addressed to the Entry Clearance Manager. They stated how she had been awarded a three-week holiday in the UK for being the year's best worker. There were covering letters for the Thai (listed as the company Human Resources Manager) who would accompany her to the Embassy. There were details of her finances.

Charli continued her search through the filing cabinets. She scanned letters to Chiang Mai, letters from Chiang Mai,.to and from Chiang Rai. Nearly always to Thai counterparts, but often to Chinese names - ex Kuomintang. All the names were cryptic nicknames. Usually, the names of the Chinese were family names. Not the usual translation to Thai. Details in the letters were also cryptic. In a file marked 'UK' there were a series of sub files. Letters to UK businessmen and companies and a set to a prominent Labour MP in Yorkshire. Robert Ferguson was one of the champagne socialists, noted Charli.

Charli was familiar with him. She recalled his insincere smile when she had met him at a party several years back. The MP was supposedly happily married but Charli knew of his penchant for gay orgies. She wondered what she should do with this additional evidence of his involvement in the world of drug smuggling. Some businessmen Charli knew. Ferguson was, at first, a surprise. But the more she thought of him, the more she could believe he would be involved in this kind of business. A smarmy self-important image-conscious man of the nineties. Impeccably dressed with a façade of caring. With these letters, Charli could cause major rumbles throughout the British business and political establishment. Steven Hunt had influential friends in prominent places. In the UK and in Thailand. And probably also in the other countries that he appeared to frequent.

It was clear to Charli that when the police, Smith especially, got close to one of his aliases, he would retire that alias and establish a new one. This had happened just after Christmas of last year for 'Simon Barrington'. Charli noted that the one name he never used was Steven Hunt. This she now assumed to be his real name.

She held the UK file in her hand and considered what to do with it. She could destroy many people with this. Many people who deserved to be destroyed. Charli took the file into the comfort of the lounge and read the many letters. Both 'To' and 'From' Steven Hunt's various aliases. There was a threatening letter from Ferguson warning Hunt to keep his mouth shut. This one letter would destroy him and get him a richly-deserved prison sentence. She closed the file and studied the letter for a further few minutes. And then she put the letter back in its place, walked back to Steven Hunt's study, and returned the file to its place in the cabinet.

There were details of accounts. Many bank accounts and in different names. Gustav Lund, Simon Barrington, Julian Wexley, Charles Harris. Charles Harris? Large amounts of money. Details of transfers to the UK, to Switzerland, The Bahamas, Jersey, Hong Kong, Singapore, Lagos, the list went on. Everything put together told the full story to Charli.

Charli took the diaries and moved back into the lounge. She turned off the light of his study but left the door open. Hungry, she went to the fridge and looked inside. There was little to eat. She found some crisps and walked back into the lounge. She moved to the telephone and saw the directory. The reception desk in the lobby could order in food from some local restaurants, Charli ordered a cheeseburger.

Eating the crisps and drinking the wine, Charli made notes from the diaries. Dates and quotes. A pattern emerged that involved Steven Hunt, Leung-Choo, and a Patpong bar. Mister Leung was clearly the owner of the bar. He was also involved in import and export. Of many things. Mostly from the north of Thailand, especially large pieces of furniture. There were details of meetings with other businessmen. These were always at downtown Chinese restaurants in large hotels. She noted the hotels. Interestingly, he never made drug deals at Charli's Hotel. This was clearly the legal side of his business. This was Steven Hunt, the honest businessman.

Charli saw her name appear several times. She went back to his office. She continued to leaf through the filing cabinets. There was so much here for her to look at. She went to the computer and was about to turn it off. It would not be necessary to work the password. There was enough for Charli's purposes just in the filing cabinets. However, on a whim, she tried one password; HEROIN. She had expected no response, but when she saw the familiar logo flash up, she knew she had hit the jackpot and that this was the BIOS password that he had selected for his computer. Charli switched off the machine, content with her minor triumph.

In a file labelled 'SITES' she found hand-drawn maps of minor roads. She took the Thailand road map and matched these up as best as possible. The marked sites were for obscure villages in the far north that were always off main highways. Someone clearly detailed them for him. Some were photocopies. Written in Thai but with English translations.

The bell rang. Charli quickly switched off the light and went to the door. The boy had her cheeseburger and she gave him 500 Baht and told him to keep the change. He left. Charli put the burger in the lounge and went back to the office. She made a note of locations and dates. She had what she wanted. She could sleep easily tonight. But for now, she continued to search. It was 10.30. For the next hour, she looked through the filing cabinets but found little else that immediately interested her.

Charli took papers to the lounge and read these while eating the burger and drinking the wine. She made further notes. She corroborated letters with diary entries. Hunt clearly had a few small companies. There were some office addresses and there were business contacts. There were meetings. An hour later, she cleared everything away. There was nothing else in his office that interested her. She had found what she had come here for. The police, if ever they got their hands on this information, would be very pleased. But that was their search, not hers.

Charli was about to close the room for good when she had a sudden change of mind. She turned the light back on, looked about the room, and her thoughts went back to Lek. With an exaggerated hurry, she went back to the computer. Charli noted it had an external memory drive connected and as she turned the computer back on, she switched this on as well. She typed the six-letter password and waited while the computer powered itself up.

She clicked on 'My Documents' and looked at their properties. There was 87MB of information. On a whim, she searched to see if there were any documents or spreadsheet files hidden elsewhere on the computer. There were not. Using the search facility, she noted he kept many of his files ordered in much the same way as he maintained his filing cabinet. Headings were often the same. However, just a simple look told her that his hard disk contained more information about his activities than the filing cabinets did. There were references to *HEROIN* and also *COCAINE*. Unlike his filing cabinet, the hard disk also contained all the information on his London activities and his Colombian activities. She clicked on the Microsoft Schedule and found that he maintained several files that contained far more information than his hand-written diary entries. She saw laboratory reports, chemical analyses, prices, and much more.

She opened the box of external memory discs and selected one, placing it into the drive. She deleted its contents. For safety, she selected another disc and cleared this before making a second copy of 'My Documents'. The entire operation had taken more than an hour. During this time, Charli finished her hamburger and finished the wine. She got another bottle of wine from his fridge to celebrate. When she had finally copied all of his files, she clicked on 'My Documents' and deleted all its contents. When this was done, she closed down all the programmes she had opened and logged off the computer.

As the screen went blank, Charli turned back to the computer and once more powered it up. Before allowing Windows to kick in, Charli entered the BIOS set-up routine. From here, she selected 'change password'. Charli kept the six letters of Hunt's preferred password but added a seventh. The letter E. She confirmed the password - HEROINE - before finally closing everything down.

Finally, Charli turned her attention back to the filing cabinet. She emptied all the files that had significant information and put these in a pile on his desk. She had little idea of what she would do with the files and the disks, but she wanted them with her. She turned to his bedroom and found a large sport bag that would hold the paperwork. Charli transferred all the files and his diaries to the holdall. She rearranged his bookshelf so that Djoi would not immediately notice the missing diaries. If, indeed, she was allowed into this room.

Finally, Charli cleared her dishes and the glasses. At just before two in the morning, she went to sleep. In his room. It had been a long day.

.

Chapter 15

Charli awoke instinctively at six as the sun rose. She dozed on and off until nearly eight and then got up. She showered and dressed, then she made some tea and tidied up around his bedroom. She left it obvious that she had slept in his bed, but she wanted the maid to know that she had made some attempt to tidy up after herself.

Charli finished the tea and cleaned the cup. She wrote a note to the maid apologising for the mess. There was, however, no mess. She told the maid that Mister Steven had not returned last night. She then carefully printed the letter in a style that she did not use and signed it 'Love Sal'. On a whim Charli added a PS.

HERE'S 10,000BHT FOR YOUR STUDIES. GOOD LUCK FOR YOUR FUTURE.

Checking the apartment for one last time, Charli left. Nobody looked up as she walked across the lobby with the heavy sport bag and out into the early morning heat and dust of the city. One more anonymous soul amongst eight million.

Charli was back in her hotel room by nine-thirty. She showered and washed her hair. She wanted to take away the smell of Hunt's bathroom. Of him. She phoned room service to ensure that her travel hamper was ready.

She had just begun to dry her hair when the telephone rang. An enthusiastic Jay told her she was at a loose end and was wondering if Charli wanted to have lunch with her. Jay mentioned she had been calling for a few days now; her voice sounded concerned. She qualified matters by saying that she had to meet her father in the afternoon and needed somebody to speak to first. A friend. He had found that one of his guns was missing and he was, naturally, holding Jay responsible. He had shouted at Jay the night before and she was still hurting. Charli thought briefly. This had disturbed her plans but...

Charli told Jay that she had just got back to her hotel and that she was in between business meetings. She also told Jay that she would love to have lunch with her. Steven Hunt would just have to wait. She told Jay that she just had to fix herself and suggested they meet in the lobby bar at eleven-thirty.

Charli got dressed carefully. She made her face up before applying purple nail varnish. Content with her appearance, she picked up her purse and the complimentary newspaper, and left her room. Waiting by the lift, Charli saw a family approach. They were arguing amongst themselves. When they saw Charli, they stopped their whispered argument. She stared at them. Her lift arrived and they held back rather than take the same lift. As the doors closed, Charli grinned to herself at the family's obvious discomfort. She was feeling light-headed; almost drunk with her new power.

I think I'm beginning to love this. I'm finally free.

The lift doors opened, and she breezed into the lobby. Heads turned. Charli was aware of this. There were many times when she wanted to make herself as invisible as possible. But this was not one of those times. Instead, she was content to present as high a profile as possible. She walked into the lobby bar and stood waiting until a waitress came over. Charli sat down, ordered a glass of wine and started to read her newspaper. Surprisingly, Jay arrived on time. As Jay ordered a whisky and soda, Charli commented on her punctuality.

"Bloody traffic, Charli. You can never rely on it. I told you I'd see you at eleven-thirty, so I expected to get here about twelve or twelve-fifteen. I left at eleven, expecting it to take an hour. Traffic was a breeze, so I got here early. Early for me anyway."

Charli could not help but laugh at this Bangkok logic. Jay continued.

"Hey, you're in a perky mood. I think I can count on the fingers of one hand the number of times I've seen you laugh since I met you. What's brought this on?"

"Oh, well, I don't know. Many things. It's too much for me to explain."

"Well, whatever you're on, Charli, keep taking it. I've never seen you looking so alive. And the make-up, the nail varnish. My God, this is almost a new Charli. You look stunning. Not that you don't usually. You are putting me even further into the shadow, which is something you know I don't like. You bitch."

The ever-effervescent Jay leaned forward and kissed Charli.

Charli had not been aware of any change in her condition, but it was obvious now that something had altered if others could see a difference. At the back of Charli's mind was Jay's comment about the missing gun. She wanted to know details but was too cautious to raise the subject with Jay.

"How did your trip to Khao Yai go? Did you let him get his leg over? Did he finally get to bang you? Is that why we've made the change?"

Charli had forgotten that Jay knew about the trip to Khao Yai with Hunt. In her reply, she made a mistake.

"Oh, it didn't come off Jay. We were supposed to go a few days ago, but he never turned up. Probably had to buzz off up-country at the last minute. Steven's pretty unreliable like that. The shit."

Jay looked quizzically at her friend.

"Oh? It's just that I phoned the hotel the other day and they said you'd left with him. They said you went off with a picnic hamper. I thought, how romantic after all you'd said about him before."

Charli was angry at this intrusion into her affairs. She was especially angry at herself for having slipped up so badly. She told herself to stick to the truth as far as possible. It was always much less trouble.

The gun. What about your father's gun?

"You win, Jay. We had a few quiet days away. That's all I'm prepared to say. Nothing happened if you're wondering. He's been working on me for three years and he will not get his leg over that quickly, if ever. And now he's gone up north some place. Some hellhole. Can we leave Steven out of this for now?"

"Oh, bloody hell, Charli, you're no fucking fun. That's the sole reason I wanted to come over. Girl talk, you know? I wanted the gory details. How big is his dick? Does it bend to the right or left? Is he chopped? Does he dive straight in or does he treat you tenderly? You know, that kind of thing. It would've helped me take my mind off dealing with Father this afternoon. Still, now I know the reason for your sudden transformation. It must be love."

Let's get off this subject, please. If you only knew the gory details, you would not be speaking to me like this.

"Say, do you want to go out for a meal this evening?"

"I can't. There are things I need to do out of town for a few days. I'll call you in a day or two when I get back and we can go out then. Then I'll have everything cleared, I promise."

"Out of town? Okay, I'll see you then. Maybe you'll be readier to talk. Because there's a lot we need to discuss. Now I must go and apologise to Father. I really was fucking shitty to him last night and I wish I could've taken the words back straight away. His beloved Beretta's gone missing, and he blamed me again. Anything goes wrong or anything disappears: blame Jay. She must've done it.

"When I was about sixteen, I took one of his guns for a bit of private target practice. Accidentally shot a neighbour's dog in its back leg. Never did like the thing, anyway. It used to crap outside our gate. Walked with a limp ever after and would never come near me again. I yelled at Father that it wasn't me this time. A Beretta's a bloody heavy handgun and I don't think I could handle one. One shot and I'd probably land flat on my cute little Thai ass. I told Father this, and then, speaking of cute little Thai asses, I told him to see if it was one of his boyfriends."

Charli looked surprised at this. Jay noticed.

"Oh Charli, you hadn't realised. Father's gay. Surely, you'd realised that. Anyway, I shouldn't have said that to him. It was crass of me."

Charli looked long and hard at Jay in a new light. Suddenly she realised what she had been missing all this time. About Djim, Yai, Jay, and John. Especially John. For a while longer, she continued to stare into Jay's face.

Father. My father. Yai is not your real father.

"My God, no. I hadn't realised Yai was gay. Not that it matters, but... but now that explains things. Look Jay. When I get back, I want to have a meal with you. And John? I need to talk to you both."

"Oh, sorry Charli. I thought you knew. Didn't you hear? Oojay got recalled to London quickly. There was a small emergency with his medical consultancy that only he could handle. He went back last night. Didn't he leave a message?"

Charli felt hurt that he had left no message for her. But she said nothing. She picked up the bill and signed it while Jay headed off to Yai's office to make her apology. As Charli watched Jay breeze out of the hotel, she went to the front desk. She asked if there had been any messages for her. The boy on the desk checked her key-drop and said there was nothing. A cashier looked across and spoke.

"Yes, Miss Charli. Yesterday there was one man he leave the message. He ask especially for it to be placed in your room. Not in the key-drop."

Charli thanked the woman and rushed back to her room. Throwing open the door, she checked behind it before noticing the envelope on the writing table. She tore it open.

Charli, I'm dreadfully sorry for this mess. A hospital in Birmingham that I have a lucrative contract with faxed me with a problem. It was impossible to clear the problem for them from Bangkok. I had to get a flight back as soon as possible so I could see them Sunday morning. They're a very lucrative client. It's contracts like these that keep my Rolls Royce on the road and my chauffeur employed. I'm sure you understand.

Before I left, I had a long session with Yai, jay, and Grandma Djim. I'll leave it to them to talk to you. Yai and Jay (and no doubt GD) will help you, I know. But trust me, you have my support also. It's what families are for.

I recall you saying at some point about returning to London next week. Give me a call and we'll meet up for dinner. There'll be much to discuss, I know.

Good luck for the future.

With love

John

Charli was stunned. The note was so ambiguous. She read it several times, trying to discern the meaning. She wondered if there was any way that they were aware of what she had done with Hunt. She concluded that this was impossible. But why would she need their support? Especially the support of Yai, whom she had little contact with. Grandma Djim had been added as an afterthought.

Charli did not care for this surprise. It complicated an already problematic period in her life. Looking back on her conversation with Jay, she realised Jay had other things on her mind. Things Charli knew she wanted to talk about. She grabbed a bag and took out the small piece of paper with Jay's mobile telephone number on it. It was a long shot because she knew that Jay usually kept the telephone turned off. It surprised her when the signal rang and when Jay answered.

"Hello Charli, I guessed somehow it'd be you. It's John's note, isn't it?"

Charli was angry now.

"Oh, it's John now. What the fuck is this all about, Jay? Tell me now."

"Didn't Oojay tell you in his note?"

"No, Jay. Oojay did not. So how about you telling me?"

"Oh Christ."

The line crackled, and Charli guessed Jay was travelling in traffic.

"I'm sorry, Charli. Can't you put your business off and see me this afternoon? I'll explain everything."

"That's impossible, Jay. Please tell me now. I'll be back in a few days and we can meet then, but for God's sake tell me something now."

"Okay. Three days ago, Grandma Djim called the family together. Father, myself, our maid, and Oojay. In our presence, and in the presence of our lawyer, she revised her will. She's left everything to you. And I mean everything, Charli."

Charli felt faint. She had been standing by the bed, but she now semi-collapsed on to it. Her skin went cold and goose bumps came up on her arms. She sat staring into the distance trying to move her mouth to speak.

"Charli, are you still there?"

After a further silence, Charli spoke.

"Everything, Jay? What does that mean?"

"Oh Christ, Charli. I don't know. I'd hoped that Oojay would've told you. He's better at these things. I'd hoped he'd sit down and talk with you about this directly. I'd expected to stay out of this. You know me. I'm too frivolous for such seriousness. As long as I've got my credit card. Are you sure you can't put off your business?"

"No, Jay, I can't. Now more than ever before. But when we get back, we need to talk. I must talk with Grandma Djim. Will you arrange that?"

"No, Charli, I can't. That's impossible. There's one more thing - even Oojay doesn't know yet. That evening, Grandma Djim didn't sleep. She spent the whole night putting everything in order and writing letters to you. I have them at home. There're about thirty pages and I don't envy you trying to decipher her scrawl. I found her, Charli, in the morning when I took her some tea. The doctor thinks she'd already been dead for maybe four hours. She had a stroke or a heart attack. It's all yours now. If it's any consolation, you've my full support. You also have Father's support. And I'm certain you have Oojay's support. It's a small family, Charli. Welcome to it. Only one person refused to join it fully. My mother."

Charli was again stunned into silence.

"What, Jay, exactly is all mine?"

"Exactly? It's too complicated to go into now. We'll tell you when you get back. But the bottom line is about two point five billion Baht, about a hundred million dollars."

Charli could not get the thought of John's note and the conversation with Jay out of her mind. She kept the note on the passenger seat, reading it whenever she had the chance. She had scribbled on the bottom of the note the figure 100,000,000. She put the commas in especially to more fully grasp the significance of the number.

Charli reached the part of the forest where a small river flowed under a bridge. She got out of the car, leaving the engine idling, and walked to the edge of the bridge. She stared down at the dormant river with its black, stagnant pools of water before looking along it to a bend that disappeared into the forest. Hunt was about one kilometre away. Hopefully dead. Sunlight reflected off the lens of a shattered camera. She turned her back on the camera, on him and on the river. She was at peace. The tone of the engine changed as the air-conditioning timer switched back on. Charli pushed herself away from the edge of the bridge and went back to the car.

It was now late afternoon. Charli had thought about walking through the forest to see him. Hopefully dead. That had been her initial plan until Jay had telephoned. But now, with the note from John and the news from Jay, she had other things on her mind. She got back into the car and turned it back onto the road. She drove north, out of the park, and back to a hotel that she had stayed in with Lek a few years ago.

CHAPTER 16

Following a good night's sleep that had few dreams, Charli awoke. She showered and dressed for the day ahead. She drove back into the park and stopped the car in her now familiar spot.

Charli sorted out all that she wanted for this day. She glanced at her watch. It was almost ten-thirty. She moved through the forest, following what was now becoming a familiar trail for her. The forest was quiet. There was evidence it had rained the previous night. She stopped and listened. She could not hear the insects. Even the birds were silent.

It was not easy for Charli to be unsettled, but she was now. A breeze was blowing through the tops of the trees. She looked around her to determine what was wrong. The forest was different. This was not like the last few days. As she looked around, she noticed the leaves were moist. And the fallen leaves did not crackle as before when she walked on them. She looked down at her feet and saw the tiny but distinctive movement of a leech that was crawling towards her. Before the hungry animal could reach Charli, she carried on walking to the river.

When Charli arrived at the open area of the river bed, there was a difference there as well. Instead of the burst of sunlight that had greeted her the last few days, there was a diffused light and silence. She put her bag down and moved cautiously into the middle of the river bed toward the hole. Charli looked around her. She had thought that escape would be impossible. She moved cautiously to the hole and peered slowly over its edge. Hunt was crumpled in the bottom of the hole. He was in the foetal position.

She took a fallen branch with her and prodded him with the stick. She was hoping he was dead. The body at the bottom of the hole groaned. Slowly, he turned his face upwards. His movements were laboured. A combination of the damaged limbs and the stiffened joints because of the cold and damp. He gazed at her through barely aware eyes. He raised a hand to shield his eyes from the diffuse light which silhouetted her beautiful but now, to him, awful face. His hair was matted. His hands were blackened and his fingernails were torn. He coughed and then winced at the pain this caused in his infected chest. There was no strength in his voice. He rasped and tried to clear his throat before speaking. But even this act caused him pain.

"Get me out of here, Charli. Please. Please get me out."

"It rained, Charli. In the night, it rained. And again this morning."

He coughed, and in the fit, his head hit the wall of the hole. Blood oozed from this newly open wound on his brow.

"I'm cold. Cold and wet. It rained on me and I have a fever. I'm dying, Charli and it's you that's killing me."

He coughed again. He hit his head once more against the wall. He appeared to be beyond any sense of caring.

For Charli, the rain from the previous night now explained why the forest was quiet. Apart from intermittent showers, the forest had been dry for several months. Dry and largely quiet. But now the forest was awaking with the start of another wet season. Part of the continual cycle. This was probably why it all sounded so different to her as she had walked through the forest just a few minutes before.

"I'm so sorry it rained on you, Steven. Did you know; that's not supposed to happen for another few weeks yet. Oh well, never mind. The best laid plans of mice, men, and little old me."

She smiled down at him. He looked up at her, searching for something in the shadows on her face. But there was not any sign on her face that she wanted to help him. And that he found horrifying.

"Fucking hell, Steven. Can you give me that look again? It looks just like those refugees that stare into the cameras of photojournalists who tour African countries and Asian flood disaster areas. Do it again, just for me."

"Fuck you, Charli."

"Haven't you always wanted to, Steven? I saw your diaries the other night."

He started at this. In his state of increasing confusion, Hunt had forgotten that she had told him she was going to Bangkok to his apartment. He had lost track of time. He was unaware that he had already spent a whole day on his own in the forest. It was almost two days since he had spoken with Charli.

"I don't believe you, Charli. Djoi would not have let you in."

"Oh, she did, Steven. She let me in. For 4000 thousand Baht, she went off because you and I were supposed to be having a quiet, intimate night in together. Only you didn't make it. I don't know why. 'Sal' left her a note to say you'd not come back. I don't know, maybe you were seeing another girlfriend. Were you, Steven? Were you being a naughty two-timer? A butterfly?"

"She told me you normally only gave her two hundred Baht. Who do you usually bring back? I'm intrigued. Bar girls? You'd never get past first base with most Thai women. Your sort can only succeed if they fucking well pay for it. Djoi told me you paid her off a lot when you brought girls back. But how many were for sex? And how many were for the purpose you took my Lek back for? I wonder. She did go back to your place? Didn't she?"

"Fuck you, you lesbian bitch."

"That, Steven, is so you. Your predictable fall back with me. Lesbian bitch. Lesbian this. Lesbian that. What, on this god-forsaken planet, makes you assume I'm a lesbian? The simple fact I wouldn't hop in to your bed at the first opportunity? Is that it? Is that why I must be a lesbian? Because I've refused the undoubted joy of being fucked by the Great Stud Steven?"

She laughed at him, shaking her head.

"You couldn't be more wrong, Steven. I'm not a lesbian."

"You've been chasing me for three years now. You never pushed the right buttons. You just always assumed I was playing hard to get. And when I appeared too hard to get, you wrote me off as a lesbian. Just to protect your fractured, fucking male ego. How wrong. How fucking wrong."

"I really am now hard to get. Now I'm fucking impossible to get. For you or any other man. Or woman, for that matter. Nobody, Steven, can have me now, or in the future. That's all finished. But in the past, Steven? The right words would've got you what you wanted."

Charli laughed at him again. Her mocking laughter drilled into his head through his one functioning ear. All that he could hear or feel was the throbbing pulse and a dull ache that seemed to eat into his brain like maggots.

"Steven? Hello? Steven? Is there anybody in? Look at me."

He turned his head slowly up to face her.

"The right words, Steven. You could've had, you could've got what you wanted. I can't believe the irony, even now. You threw away Lek to go after me."

Charli continued laughing and moved away from his hole. He could not see her. She came back with a cold beer and a bottle of Glenfiddich whisky. She cracked the seal and unscrewed the lid of the whisky, guessing he would not have the strength, and dropped the bottle into his lap.

"Here Steven. If you're cold after last night's rain, this'll warm you up. Think of me as some sloppy-floppy Saint Bernard in the Alps."

She let her tongue hang out and panted in a ludicrous imitation of a dog.

As he took hold of the bottle, he looked up and saw her give a toothy, animated grin. Charli went silent. She drank her beer and sat near the hole, staring at the forest that surrounded her. He looked up at her but could not see her face. Only the outline of her chin silhouetted against the clouded grey sky. She looked down into the dark and damp hole. His huddled body was nursing the bottle of whisky. He brought it to his lips and drank. Spilling some on his now badly soiled and torn silk shirt. Hunt whimpered to himself, pathetically.

"Why this? Why Charli? What've I done to you to deserve this? I keep asking myself and I keep asking you and you won't tell me. I've never had you. I've never hurt you. So why me?"

The muscle twitched again in Charli's neck. She glanced down at him. She said nothing for a while. She merely looked at the broken body that stared up, pathetically, at her.

"Why you? Because, Steven, you deserve it. There're plenty of men who have done far more damage physically and emotionally, far more hurt and given far more suffering to me. But finally, I've got one of the untouchables. I've got you. You've glided through life like some absolute untouchable. But I know the misery you've caused. I know because I've seen it close up. I've smelt the death you bring to others. I've lived with it. You've walked effortlessly between the rain drops without so much as a polluting drip of acid rain touching you."

Hunt gathered some strength and raged at her.

"You know nothing, Charli, nothing."

"I've been in your study, Steven. In your filing cabinets, in your computer. There was enough there to confirm my suspicions. There's much more that I could have read. Enough for me to slot every little fucking thing into its little place. And there was your computer, Steven. Good idea to lock it up with a BIOS password. But it wasn't difficult to realise what you used. H.E.R.O.I.N. That was pretty fucking stupid, Steven. It was the first I tried. And you know what the second would've been? C.H.A.R.L.I. I bet you alternated those."

"You've glided between, and no doubt through, the police forces of the world conducting your business of death and getting rich on it. You've thought nothing of the consequences down the line.

And you've the gall to whine in your hole to me. Why me?"

Charli's tone was a mocking one.

"Because, Steven, I know your business. I've seen the end fucking result of your fucking business. I've seen the end fucking results of the turbo-charged Lotus payments you boasted about a few years ago. And I've now had the misfortune to see it twice. The first time was bad enough. Christ, was it bad? But now? The second time? Now I thought I'd finally left all that behind me. I do not know whether you had any hand in Kim's death. That was almost eight years ago. You probably didn't."

"But I know one thing. I can hold you responsible for Lek's death. And I do. It was you who filled her body with the heroin that killed her. Yet still you ask, why me?"

CHAPTER 17

Charli got up and walked away from the river. She took another bottle of beer from the bag and opened it as she continued to walk into the forest. She was trembling with pent-up rage. She walked away from the usual trail, the trail that went back to the road. She walked further into the forest, exploring the trees and the plants about her. It had always surprised her how relatively clear of undergrowth tropical forest was. It was not as she had been led to believe from the movies.

There were small saplings four- or five-feet-tall waiting to take their place in the upper canopy. Between some of these were the giant webs of equally giant forest spiders. The black, red, and yellow ones that had spooked Hunt a few days before. Charli also was wary of them. Not because she was particularly scared of spiders. She was not. A long time ago, she had made friends with a spider. It had been her companion in troubled times. She was wary because when she walked into their six-foot diameter webs she was caught up in thick sticky gossamer which turned to a yellow goo on her face. A yellow goo that matted in her hair.

Charli continued walking further into the forest. Looking for a rock to sit on or a fallen tree. After a few minutes, she found a fallen tree. As she sat, she looked back at the path she had followed. The path was not there. She was breathing heavily now. Many years' worth of rage was finally building to a climax. Charli drank her beer and stared along the line of the moss-covered, recently fallen tree. A single orchid which had spent its entire life high above the forest floor was now struggling to live its last months on the fallen trunk of the tree, which was already being invaded by a new inventory of plants. Plants more used to the competition of the dark, dank forest floor. Charli looked at the tiny yellow and white nutant flowers that moved in some imperceptible breeze. A final flowering. A final dispersal of seeds for another generation before its death. She bent over to pick the tiny flower. Cradling it in her fingers for the briefest of moments, she changed her mind and let it go to live out the short remains of its life in peace.

Ten years before, Charli had hoped that someone might come and save her. For a very brief while, she had tried to convince herself that what was happening to a 13-year-old girl was all a terrible dream. But no child could possibly dream what she was experiencing. Every hour of her day waking and sleeping had become a nightmare. Charli thought dispassionately about predicaments: Kim's, Wessel's, Lek's, her own past, and Hunt's present.

She would not bother asking him what was going through his mind. Because nobody had ever thought to ask her. She had not been important 10 years ago. And now, he was not important. Charli Harris had been stripped of her dignity and humanity and now so was Hunt. She was merely going to make him aware of why he had to die. As she drank from the bottle and continued to look about her, she saw the moss and algae covered bones of a forest animal. Close by were the corroding, discarded batteries of a torch. The forest had many poachers. Paid by big businessmen to get exotic foods for select restaurants in Bangkok. Death was everywhere. Charli looked at the tree that she had been sitting on. It had been a large and strong tree in its day. She patted its moss-covered trunk as she stood up from it.

"Thank you. I hope when you fell you didn't kill your daughter - unlike my father."

Charli made a wai to the tree before walking off. She picked her way back through the forest. There was no discernible path. Instinct told her where to go. Back to the river. Back to Hunt. Back to the turning point in her still, short life.

When she reached the river, she could hear his plaintive wailing. She walked carefully back to the hole until she was close enough to listen to him. She sat on a rounded boulder of the river bed and listened. He mumbled incoherently. She found it difficult to understand what he was saying. After a few minutes, she moved to the edge of the hole and peered in.

At her movement, he looked up.

"For fuck's sake Charli. Help me. It hurts."

"What hurts, Steven?"

"Everything Charli. Every fucking thing. You did this to me and now I'm pleading with you. For pity's sake. Stop this sadistic madness and help me. I told you I loved you. I still do. But you've got to help me before it's too late. I was going to change my life just for you. Don't you understand?"

Charli stared at him. What he now saw frightened him further. For there was nothing. No emotion.

"You've been hurting for a few days, Steven. How old are you? Thirty-nine, I think you said. Forty? A few days out of 39 fucking years. What about me? What about the hurt I've had? Ten years, Steven. Nearly half of my fucking life, Steven. So, do not expect any pity from me. I've no pity left to give. I've been dehumanised. If not by you directly, then certainly by your kind. I can't help you, Steven. Only you can do that. You shouldn't have got yourself into this hole in the first place."

He mustered up some anger once again.

"Fucking hell, Charli. I didn't do this to me. You did. You crazy bitch. You fucking shot me. You fucking pushed me in here."

"Wrong, Steven. Wrong, wrong, wrong, wrong. You're a businessman. You've spent three years trying to impress me. You forget. I went to your apartment last night - the other night. I know your business."

"I've told you. You know nothing Charli, nothing."

"You've told me in the past about your trade in cut flowers, in toys, in furnishings, computers, software. Your work for KA holdings. In this, that, and the other. Why did I not see any evidence of these last night, the other night, Steven? Why? At your apartment. In your study. There was no evidence of that side of your business. Four filing cabinets and nearly a hundred megabytes of computer files. Nothing. Why? Because your offices for your cover business are down in Silom. At the headquarters of KA. And at my hotel. The hotel where we've met so often. That hotel is a front for you, isn't it?"

"What I saw in your apartment was your real business in Thailand. The real money-maker. Drugs, Steven. And lots of them. I'd not realised before how cynical you people are. Christ, I thought I was cynical. But your diary showed it. Hell, Steven. How can you have such little regard for human life? Pat, Patsy, P, Phee. What else've you used? Patty, Patricia, Tricia, Trixie? At the end of the day, they all derive from Patsy. And what is a Patsy, Steven? The world's most famous Patsy was Lee Harvey Oswald. You should know that. But your diary is full of other patsies. I don't know who they are. Or were. Except for one. Except for one, Steven."

"Last year, Steven, your diary is full of entries for your help for 'Pat'. On December 10, you even said that you helped 'Pat' pack. Twenty-four little hours later, Steven, 'Pat' was dying horribly in a hospital in a foreign country. Far from the country of her birth. And, much more importantly, far from her land of birth from the soil. Far also from her ancestors. And you were the cause, Steven. You helped her 'pack'. Along with Choo. What you packed her with killed her. You killed my fucking friend."

"Did she have problems swallowing the condoms, Steven? 'Pat' was my friend Steven. 'Pat' was Lek. A go-go dancing prostitute from a Patpong bar run by your fucking business partner, Mister Leung – Choo."

"And now you ask me 'why?'. 'Why me Charli'?'"

Charli's tone was once again mocking. Hunt groaned now at the awful realisation that Charli really did know all about his business. All these years he had successfully kept everything so secret from those that did not need to know. Linda had accidentally got close. And he had arranged a fatal accident for her, one that turned out horribly messy.

"You ask 'why?' Steven. Because she was one of the few friends I had. I had plans to help her. To look after her, to give her a new start. Lek wasn't very capable of making a break on her own, she wasn't that bright. She needed help and guidance. And you killed her, Steven. 'Why me Charli?' That's why. You killed my one fucking friend."

"Oh Christ, Charli. You did get into my study? You really managed to get in."

"I told you I would, Steven, that I could. And I did. Yes, I'm resourceful. Very fucking hugely resourceful. My upbringing taught me to be. But also, in another life, I was made to take an IQ test. One-five-three is one fuck of a burden to carry, I can tell you – at any level in our sordid fucking society. It's not something I'd wish on anybody. I'm one fucking clever cunt, Steven. Too clever by a long trip to the moon and back for you."

"I spent the evening putting everything together. I couldn't get into your computer at first. But it wasn't necessary. There was more than enough to convince me I'd done the right thing. You wouldn't believe what I found. Or perhaps you would. It was your office, after all. Hell, Steven, you're well connected. Big industrialists in Britain and in Thailand. Thai MPs, Thai police, Thai army, and Thai businessmen I'd expected. After all, they're all rolled into one big corrupt mess. But you even have a British MP. Though I must admit, it didn't surprise me to see Bob Ferguson in league with you. I met him once. The public-school educated, Oxbridge-acceptable face of socialism always came across to me as something of a fraud. Thai police generals, I expect. But British bobbies as well? Our Boys in Blue? I'd not fully understood how far all of this went. The one thorn, judging from your diaries, appears to have been our mutual friend Derek Smith. I found stuff linking you with high-ups in the US Drug Enforcement Agency. And I'd thought they were incorruptible."

Charli leafed through her notebook. She read out names for Hunt. He realised, now, finally, how serious his situation was. If any of this information leaked out, there were many people who would have him on a hit-list.

"Now there's a joke. If I want, I could blow the lid on everything. Maybe I will. I haven't quite decided yet. I copied all of your files to those external storage discs just to be safe. They're neat. I like them. I'll probably spend a few pleasant evenings going through everything at leisure and then I'll decide what to do. Last night, however, I decided that my life has to finish here, Steven. And then I have to start again. It's 'kind of a Buddhist thing', as our trippy Californian cousins might say. If I got involved in exposing all I could, I'd never be free. Sorry to say, Steven. I'm no hero. No heroine. Or is that heroin?"

"I want everything to finish here and now, so I can start again. Phoenix from the ashes. You get the picture? I'm doing this last thing for Kim, for Lek, and for me. Can you understand that? After ten years, I want the fucking nightmares to stop Steven. They've been going on now for too long. Ten fucking years I've gone to sleep wondering if it'll be sound. Sometimes it has been. Often it hasn't. They have to stop."

"You're wrong about me being mad. I'm not mad, Steven. But if I don't clear everything, if the nightmares don't stop, then I surely will go mad. Because I can't take too much more for too much longer. I want to be free, Steven. And you'll help me. Do you understand?"

Charli looked down at him. At one time, an age ago, Hunt had seemed so confident. But now he was not so self-assured. Now he had been put in his place. And that place was a seven-foot deep hole in a dried river bed in a tropical forest far from anywhere. And more importantly, far from anyone that could help. Hunt coughed and tried to adjust his position to make himself a little more comfortable.

"It'll be getting dark soon, Steven. I need to go. You wouldn't want me to get lost in the forest, would you?"

"Charli, don't leave me here again. Please. Take me with you. Help me. Whatever's happened to you in the past, it doesn't need to come to this. What you're leading up to is murder. Murder, plain and simple, Charli, if you let me die here… Okay, I accept you know my business. What'll it take? How much money? Please tell me and I'll do anything, I promise. You know so much about my activities I can never make any problem for you. Get me out of this hole. Get me to the hospital in Nakorn Nayok. It's only 70 kilometres away."

"We make up some story that bandits overcame us and shot me as I tried to protect you. You ran off into the forest and hid for a few days, scared, until you found me. It'll work, Charli, it will. Nobody'll ever know the truth, I promise. I really do love you. Get me out of here and I'll not make a problem for you. Tell me how much money you want and I'll give it to you, I promise. But for God's sake, just get me out of here. I don't want to die. Not in this hole. I want my life back. And you're the only person who can do that. You're the only person who can give me my life back. Please, Charli. I love you, help me."

Charli looked down at his pleading face, streaked with tears.

"The irony."

She shook her head from side to side as she said this.

"You offering me money. Now. You'll probably never get to appreciate the irony. However, not a bad idea. I'll think about it. In the meantime, I'll leave you with this other bottle. You've gone through most of that first one. I know what a comfort that can be for you, Steven. Believe me, I know. Alcohol's helped to give me a good night's sleep for most of the last ten years. You surely must've noticed I have a small alcohol problem. A day doesn't go by when I don't have some."

"If you wake up in the night, you can always have a few drinks to send you back to the land of dreams. It works wonders, Steven. Try it. If the demons haunt you in the night, fend them off with alcohol. Much more effective than garlic. Trust me on that one, that's what I used to do. That's what Kim used to do. But after a while, it got too much for Kim. After a while, she needed something a little stronger than alcohol. After a while, she had to turn to you and your kind for comfort. Do you understand now what I'm getting at?"

"Lek died with almost a kilogram of heroin inside her. And she only weighed 41 kilograms. But she was meant to be caught, wasn't she Steven? Just so the drug squad, the US DEA, the politicians, and others could say they were being vigilant. Could say they were doing their job. A few years back, there was a big fuss over two stupid girls from Birmingham. How much did they have? Sixty kilos? I wonder, were they yours, Steven? Everyone in the drug enforcement agencies crowed about what a good job they were doing. They'd caught two stupid girls. Mules with 60 kilos. Sixty kilos that failed to make it to the market. Big fucking deal, eh Steven?"

"But you know what really goes out. And you know how. And you know where. And you know when. And you know how often. And you know to whom. Not tens of kilos, Steven. Hundreds, thousands. Out through the ports. I saw the details in your files. For every shipment, Steven, how many deaths? Have you ever thought of that? Shipments-deaths. How many fucking lives have you ruined or killed?"

"I've got to go. It's getting late and I don't want to get lost in the forest. I'd hate to spend the night out here. I don't know how you do it. But that... what do we call it? Proposal? I'll give it some thought. Some consideration. So, in words you can understand I'll 'kick the idea around the ballpark' and 'get back to you on it'."

Charli shuddered in an exaggerated manner as she folded her arms about her and stared. Hunt lay huddled at the bottom of the hole. He was damp, he was cold, and his trousers and shirt were badly soiled after three days. Always fastidious about his hygiene and tidiness, this caused him almost as much distress as the bullet wounds, wounds that were now badly infected and throbbing with a life of their own.

Chapter 18

Charli picked her way through the forest in the fading light. She heard the beating of wings as a pair of giant hornbills passed overhead in the dying afternoon of the day. When Charli reached the road, she stopped as six bikes with teenagers came noisily around the slight bend. Each bike was belching blue-grey smoke from the illegally-altered exhausts. She followed the now familiar routine of keeping close to the trees and listening for traffic as she moved back to where her car was parked. Once again, she reached it with no problems. She turned the car onto the road and drove north, out of the park, and back to the hotel she had stayed at.

On reaching the hotel, she parked next to a Mercedes. There were more cars in the car park this time as it was the weekend. A sign over the hotel entrance welcomed the management of a Bangkok-based company, which was having its annual company outing. Charli knew what that would mean. No wives, no children. She guessed also that there would be no female employees, only the men. But she also guessed they would not be without female company.

Charli had deliberately chosen this hotel. She knew that in the evenings, as she sat and watched them drooling over young girls, it would harden her resolve. She had come, suddenly, to understand how closely linked drugs and prostitution were. While some might have considered it too much of a generalisation, Charli also knew that the controlling interests in these two activities were usually held by (but by no means always) men and that the victims were usually (but by no means always) women. As she sat watching them act out their pathetic lives, she knew she was doing the right thing. She had no feelings for Hunt. Ten years of this life had desensitised her.

The buffet breakfast was expensive and of poor quality. The only juices were orange or pineapple, neither of which she liked and neither of which were fresh. The eggs were not freshly cooked, as at quality hotels, but were left to go cold on the warm plates. The same for the bacon, which was streaky, very fatty, and thrown on top of pieces of toast which Charli presumed was to soak up some of the fat. Squares of anaemic ham drifted in pools of oil-laden water.

The hotel had delusions of grandeur which was reflected in its room rates, but not in the service. Profit rather than service was the bottom line in a place such as this. It was definitely, like so many in Thailand, a third - or even fourth - rate hotel pretending to be first.

The toast was cold, the butter almost liquid in its small wrapper. The eggs were rubber, the bacon shrapnel. The coffee was stewed.

She had hoped to get a paper to read but had given up. There was no Bangkok Post or The Nation. Although these papers had been present in the week, now there was only a selection of three Thai or four Chinese papers. She returned to her room and showered.

Charli was not sure why but inside; her stomach was knotted. She was tense. She showered slowly and deliberately. The water was hot and she could feel the blood rush to the surface of her skin. A pulse pumped in her temple and the bathroom felt darker. This sensation had occurred to her many times in the past and she was always worried in case she fainted. It often presaged a migraine.

Charli finished washing her hair. Starting from the top, she removed all the soapy water from her face. Then her body. Charli felt her breathing become tight, and she knew she had to get out of the shower before she fainted. Stopping the shower, she brushed the excess water from her body before stepping out. She held the towel in front of her as she looked into the steam-covered mirror. Charli had never liked brushing water from mirrors before. She did not know why. But she now made a single swipe across the glass. She stared at her face for a while as she held the towel under her chin.

The air-conditioning droned, and she had the same lost feeling that had haunted her since she was a child. Less so now, but occasionally she could stand in a crowded shopping plaza and feel nobody around her. She could watch people pass by, and through her. There was nobody in her hotel room now, but that only heightened the sensation.

She turned from the mirror and drifted into the claustrophobic room. Claustrophobic and yet empty. A contradiction? Suddenly tired and drained, she collapsed on to the bed. For a short time, Charli lay staring at the ceiling and watching a small insect crawl across its upside-down two-dimensional universe. She drifted off into a fitful sleep where she awoke constantly. And each time, there was another memory from her past. Only this time, a highly confident Thai woman and a white tiger walked through these ghost memories, showing her the way forward.

It was an hour before she gathered herself together. She sat naked in front of the mirror towelling her still damp hair and looking at the reflection. The woman who stared back at her was tired and looked a lot older than her years. There was little life in her eyes. So many times, Charli had been told that her eyes spoke volumes about her soul. As she sat looking at her reflection, she knew it was all bullshit. These were eyes that had not shed a tear in over eight years. She spoke to her reflection.

"Every one of you was full of fucking bullshit. Not one of you could ever read my eyes. None of you could ever see into my soul. You fucking bastards."

She packed her bag in a dream, checked the room, and left. After she had checked out, Charli resisted, once again, the attempts of the porters to take her bag and walked out to her car. Although it was not hot, the intense air-conditioning of the hotel made the outside feel warm and humid. She got into the car and drove off. As she left the car park, she knew she would never come back to this hotel. It had served its purpose.

Chapter 19

Charli drove rapidly through the park. Near to the headquarters there were macaque monkeys by the side of the road. A few years before, these would have scampered into the trees. Now they stood expectantly by the road, begging for food.

As she passed the visitor centre, a coachload of children was swarming around the car park. She guessed these were from one of the capital's international schools. Out here to learn about nature. Red in tooth and claw. Just like Hunt.

Charli travelled the nine kilometres passed the visitor centre, leaving that small piece of civilisation behind. She stopped the car in her usual place. She noticed that the ground was soft where it had rained again the night before. There were small puddles of water in her car tracks from the previous day's rain. She sensed the rain, but in its shyness, it had only fallen in the night time.

Charli went through the familiar routine of opening the boot and checking her rucksack. She set off down the road. Halfway to the forest trail, she heard the distant drone of a car behind her. To her right was a steep earth bank. There was no time to get into the forest. Charli threw herself down into the culvert. It was only a shallow V shape. She hoped they would not see her. If anyone saw her lying in the culvert, they would be bound to stop. The red pickup truck came speeding along, belching black smoke. She saw it clearly as it came round the bend. But she felt sure the driver would not see her. As it drew level with her, she could no longer see the pickup truck, which meant they would not see her. She held her breath as it went by, dreading the thought that it might stop. It had no reason to. The way that her car was parked, it was impossible for the pickup driver to see it from the direction he was coming. It passed and Charli listened as it changed gear and sped up the hill and into the distance. She waited for a few seconds, listening for other cars. All that she could hear was the high-pitched whine of several species of cicadas, more than in the past few days.

Charli picked herself up, brushed off the grit from the bottom of the culvert, and carried on her way. She still felt flushed, and a pulse ticked in her temple. She entered the now-familiar forest and picked her way through its damp undergrowth.

When she reached the river, she sat down on her favourite rock and surveyed the tranquil scene. All was silent. After a while, the cold wetness of the rock seeped through her skirt and wet her knickers. It had obviously rained hard in the night as it was wet everywhere.

The rocks were slippery as the dried algae had now become wet and once again brought to life. Charli moved cautiously to the edge of the hole and peered in. As she looked over the edge, she saw the familiar sight. The last few days, he had been in a foetal position. Now he was just collapsed in the bottom of the hole. She looked around and found the stick that she had used the previous day. She prodded him with it, hoping he was finally dead. As he awoke, he broke into a fit of violent coughing. His breathing was now even more laboured than the day before and he could not control himself. When he looked up at her, Charli could see that his head was badly cut and one eye was almost closed from a gash. The cuts around his shattered ear had gone septic and were oozing the yellow pus of a bacterial infection.

His voice was weak.

"Help me, Charli. I need a hospital. Take me to Nakorn Nayok. I've a fever. The sores are infected and last night I gashed my head. Help me, Charli. I love you, Charli. I really do."

This last word was drawn out. Charli looked down at him. No emotion. She said nothing but continued to stare at him. He stared back. He did not speak, but he mouthed a single word.

"Please."

Why aren't you dead?

Charli turned from the hole and walked back to her rucksack.

Chapter 20

When she returned, Charli sat down on the edge of the hole and looked down at him. His face, gazing up at her, was again pleading. She tore one page from a magazine and threw it down at him.

"Look, Steven, look at her. Look at her eyes and try to imagine what's going on in her mind, deep in her soul."

She tore another page and threw it in. And another, then another. Each time, she screamed at him to look. Five or six pages lay around Hunt in the hole. He made no effort to pick them up. Hunt was almost incapable of movement as Charli picked up the stick and jabbed him with it. Shaking with rage, she screamed at him.

"Fucking well look at the face, Steven. Look at the arms. Can you see the needle marks? Can you see the ugly black under her eyes? That's not some fucking badly applied eye shadow."

He started crying. The stick had gashed his neck, and blood was oozing from the jagged wound. It stained the dirty collar of his silk shirt red.

"I don't know, Charli. I don't know. I don't know these people. Why are you showing me these? I don't know them, I don't know."

His weakening voice trailed away.

"You don't know them? No, you don't fucking know them. But it's your fucking heroin they've shot themselves up with, you bastard. And those pictures are what they do… or did - maybe they're dead already - to make money to buy more heroin to free themselves from their miserable fucking lives. A vicious fucking circle, Steven. Created and driven by you and your kind. Drugs-sex, sex-drugs, but no fucking rock 'n roll, that's for sure."

Charli tore more pages from the magazine and threw these down at him.

"Look at her then, Steven. What do you think of her? Does she do anything for you? So young, so pert, and so fresh. Not quite like the other hard-nosed, world-weary cunts, is she?"

He made no move to pick up the newly-fallen pages. Charli took the stick again and prodded him once more with it. She screamed at him. A single drop of blood fell on to the face of a young girl who stared, with lifeless, emerald eyes, from the torn page.

"Hey, shithead. I'm talking to you, you subhuman parasite. Look at the pictures. Does she do anything for you? I want to know. Look at those deep, thoughtful green eyes. They speak volumes about her, don't they? Beautiful copper-burnished hair. Genuine copper, not from a bottle. Look at her Steven. What do you see? What do you think?"

At the description Charli had given Hunt, he was triggered to slowly pick up one of the pages. Ignoring the bloodied picture, he tried to focus on the page, and when he finally saw the deathly face staring out of the page at him, he convulsed.

"Seventeen fucking years old, Steven. Now do you understand? I was 17. And already it had been four years. I won't go into details. Look at the eyes, Steven. What do you see in those eyes? In the past, you'd always told me about my eyes. The window to my soul."

Her tone was mocking.

"What about those eyes, Steven? What do they say to you now? I want to know. Where's the fucking spark in those eyes, Steven? I've spent years looking at those pictures. Nearly every day I look at these magazines. My modelling portfolio. A tonic to remind myself of how far up, so very fucking far, I've come from so far down. I've been trying to see behind those eyes. Behind the alcohol and the drugs. Trying to understand the soul of that creature - that fucking pathetic excuse for a human being. Because, then, I was barely human. I existed from day to day like all animals do. It's the one thing that separates mankind from the rest of the animals on this miserable shitty planet as far as I am concerned. We make plans for the future. Well, I didn't. I had no fucking future to plan for."

Charli went silent for several seconds and Hunt looked up.

"No fucking future, then. Every time I look at those pictures I try to see what she, what I, was thinking then… And the frightening part is… Steven, I failed. I can't see anything there. So, please help me. You want me to help you. To take you from here. That proposal of yesterday. To the hospital in Nakorn Nayok. Look at these pictures and you help me. Tell me all about her, about me, because I'm desperate to know. I'm fucking desperate. You tell me all about me and I'll take you to your hospital."

Hunt screamed out a single word.

"No."

It was drawn out and, finally, strangled. Even after the last few days, he could not believe what he was now confronted with. He repeated the single word over and over. Each time quieter than the last. And then he collapsed over the pictures. Charli threw down four or five complete magazines.

"I'm going for a walk, Steven. Here're a few more pictures from my portfolio. I've decided I don't need them anymore. I'd give you some of my videos only we've nothing to play them on. I'm resourceful but I'm not that resourceful. This is a diary of my life if you like. And here's a bottle of whisky to cheer you up. You can't say I don't look after you. Don't worry about your stomach, Steven. The worst you can get is an ulcer. Believe me, I know. I got my first stomach ulcer when I was 15. Don't go away 'cos I'll be back."

Chapter 21

Leaving the hole, Charli walked off into the shade of the forest. At finally exposing herself to him, to the world, she had become more enraged and more certain of the last course she was to take with Hunt. Charli had kept so much secret from so many people. Not least her most recent friends, Sir John and his extended family which now, almost perversely, included her as its head. But she knew that in telling everything to Steven Hunt she would not be risking exposure to anyone else.

She sat a while, calming down. For the first time in a long while, Charli lit a cigarette. She always kept a packet with her but rarely smoked. She had not smoked regularly since she was 18. But occasionally she found the comfort of a cigarette necessary when thinking too much or facing severe stress as she was now. She was now calmly considering her next move with him. As she sat smoking, she picked at the torn flesh of her fingernail. Slowly she pulled a strip of skin away exposing a red-raw area which oozed blood from the newly-broken capillaries. After a few minutes she stubbed out the cigarette, stood up, walked back to the cool box, and removed a bottle of beer. She returned to his hole.

Charli could see that he was leafing through the magazines. She sat on the edge of the hole, but he had not noticed her. He turned the pages idly, with difficulty, while drinking from the whisky bottle.

"Good, aren't they?"

Hunt looked up with a start. Relieved that this time, she had not goaded him with the stick.

"Fucking hell Charli. I'm sorry. I didn't know. Didn't realise. How'd this happen? I mean. These're serious. This isn't Mayfair or Penthouse. How did you get involved in hard core porn? What happened?"

"What happened? Those pictures were taken when I was 17. Get that through your thick skull."

Charli stared down at him.

"Now maybe you can begin to understand. She's just a prostitute. Those words would make a great epitaph, wouldn't they? For Kim. For Lek. And for me. You warbled on the other day about Lek. A mere Patpong bar girl. How many men she might've had. Have you looked at magazines like these before, Steven? Have you thought about where the models come from? Most of the girls in those pictures, Steven. They're like me. They're like Lek. They're like Kim. We were, we are all prostitutes."

"Does that surprise you? I'm a prostitute. Just a fucking prostitute. I told you the other day, if you'd wanted me a few years ago, a few words would've worked. 'How much darlin'?' How many times have I heard that phrase? I'm not your darling. I'm not anybody's darling. But that's all it would have taken. Not now. Now, I'm untouchable. Untouchable for you or any man or woman."

"Never again, Steven. Never. I'm happily celibate now, very happily, and I plan to stay that way for the rest of my life. Believe me, it's far less fucking complicated."

"I've listened to you for three years now go on about Patpong bar girls in general and Lek in particular. I'm the same, Steven. I understand everything that goes through their minds. Everything. Because it's been through my mind a thousand times or more... And it's still going through it. Day after fucking day, I remember. There's a caseload of worms crawling in my head, I can tell you."

"One slight difference."

"Average Patpong girl? Nineteen to 25. Average length of time on the game? Two? Five years? Average number of buy-outs a month?

Five to ten. Average number of men inside them? Allowing for repeats and returns? Maybe two hundred in total."

"Most, no all, of them enter voluntarily. They're not lily-white virgins when they start. Trust me on that. They go in with eyes and legs open. Me? I had my soul torn out of me when I was 13. Thirteen fucking years young. So, anything you read in my eyes was a lie. I'm good at acting. I'm good at lying. I had to be when I had a bloated drunken slob, 30 or 40 or 50 fucking years older than me, pounding away inside my body. Almost eight years. I never kept a diary then, but I've estimated at least 2000 different men inside my body, Steven. But I never once let a single one of them into my mind. You're the first. Do you feel honoured?"

"I told you yesterday... was it yesterday? No, the day before. When you met Lek, you'd 've been far safer with her. She'd had less than ten men. Me? Two thousand. Can you imagine that, Steven? Two fucking thousand men inside me. Doing just that. Every which bloody way. I've been damaged. From the age of 13 up until just before I got the key to the door. Never been 21 before."

"HIV and AIDS? I know all about that. I read a lot. But do you know what? One thing I can't tell you; I've no idea if I'm HIV positive or not. There was a time when I was just too frightened to find out. Now? Who cares? I don't. If I have it, I have it. If it's time for me to die, it's time for me to die. So far, so good. I'm still alive and I'm still healthy. We all go some time. I've no idea if I've six months to live, six years or 60 years. God, can you imagine that? Living to eighty-three. I can't. I don't think I want to either. There's little to keep me on this planet I can tell you."

Hunt choked.

"Oh my God, no."

"Oh my God, yes. What Steven? Tell me. What have you realised?"

"I'm sorry, Charli. If I'd known… If I'd known."

"If you'd known what, Steven? What the fuck would you have done? Helped me? Counselled me? You would've rescued me? Married me? Saved me? Taught me the error of my ways? Shown me God? At one time or another, there's always been some prick prepared to offer me all those things. Or would you have given me heroin at a cut-price rate to speed me on my merry fucking way? Put me out of my fucking misery? That's your trade, after all. What, Steven? Fuck you, Steven. I've met my share of do-good men who have wanted to save my tormented soul."

"Only I can do that, Steven. Nobody else. Not you, not a priest, not John. And certainly, no fucking psychiatrist. Nobody can help me. So, don't think you can even begin to try. You're a nobody. Now I know what you've done. Now I know what your business is. Now I know you're less than human, less than nobody, less than nothing. I feel absolutely zero for you. I treat insects with more respect."

At these words, Hunt looked up at her again with dread in his eyes. Charli looked at him with an all-consuming loathing. She turned from the hole and went back to the shade. She got herself another beer.

When she got back to his hole, she looked down at him. He was again leafing through the magazines. She drank from the bottle and could feel the anger and the hatred rising once again. She picked up the stick, but then, fighting to control herself, she threw it away. Instead, she sat by the hole and lit another cigarette. Hunt was not aware of her presence until she blew cigarette smoke down to him. He glanced up at her. The first time that he had ever seen Charli smoking a cigarette. But now, nothing surprised him about this woman.

"I don't remember the exact date. But it's over 10 years ago when all this started. And now it's going to end. Ten years ago, Steven. I was 13. I'd come looking for my father. Can you believe that? I'd come looking for my father. He was all I had. My mother died in a car crash when I was about eight or nine months. Four years later, my father had lost his university lectureship, and me, because of the drinking. You see, he blamed himself for the crash."

"I never fitted in at any of the homes they sent me to. That's what coming from a broken home and having the burden of a high IQ does to you. I was always in trouble with the teachers. They didn't like the way I made up stories. I was good at inventing lives for myself. For a long time, I was Polish. Don't ask me why, but I had a thing for Poland. It seemed like an exotic country, although I had no idea where it was. I was a Polish Princess - Princess Katerina. I think that came about after reading about Anastasia in one of those Blue Book readers for children. Even when I was nine, I knew she was a fraud. The same as me. When I played with the other girls, I was picked on. So, I usually stayed on my own. I preferred it that way. Less trouble. Far less trouble. I could live in my own world where nobody could touch me or hurt me."

"I told everybody that when he was ready, my father was coming for me. I made up stories about his high-powered job in another country. I always remember mentioning America a lot. I'd heard it was the land of dreams. To a six or seven-year-old, that conjures up a shitload of possibilities. I've never been to America. And I've learned enough to realise America's a sham. It's not the land of opportunity everyone thinks it is. I never want to go there."

"I don't know how it happened. Stories spread. But one of the girls told me my father was a drunk who couldn't look after me or himself. I was told he didn't, couldn't, love me. He only loved his bottle of whisky. There was one teacher in particular who hated me. And there was one girl who also hated me; Kate Rimmer. She went to Miss Turnpike one day and said I'd told her my father was a nuclear scientist in America building bombs that would save the world from Russia."

"In class that day, Miss Turnpike gave us all a lesson in telling lies. She used me as an example. She reminded the class about the nasty man who'd been hanging round the gates of the school. She reminded the class that we'd all been warned to stay away from this man. That he was a bad man, a stranger. And we were never to talk with strangers. Did your parents ever tell you that, Steven? And then she told them all he was my father. That was cruel, for God's sake. I was reminded by her he'd been driving the car my mother died in. I was only nine-months-old, Jesus. I've no memories of my mother. And no pictures. But I've vague memories of my sad father losing himself to whisky. He tried to look after me, I know. But he failed."

"When she told the rest of the class this, I remember vividly going weak inside. I stared straight ahead at her standing in front of the green blackboard. Above her head was a white clock showing the time. Two twenty-seven. I watch the red hand march the seconds around. I felt as if I was the only one in the universe. Shaking with animal fear, I lost control I wet my knickers. I ran screaming from the building. All I could hear was laughter from the children in the class. I ran to the edge of the school field and clung to the rusted chicken-wire fence, hoping he'd be there. I screamed for him: 'Daddy, come back, please.' I remember, through my tears, screaming out 'Daddy, where are you?'. Even now, there're times when I wake screaming these words. I could remember his unshaven face. So sad. He never looked at any other children. Only at me. And when I looked at him, he would smile gently. I'd begun already to guess, or at least hope, who he was. Memories of my last seeing him two years before came back. The day they called the police to remove him from the school, I'd very nearly walked over to the fence to talk with him."

"Miss Turnpike had to drag me from the fence, peeling my fingers one by one from the chicken-wire. They were cut and pieces of rusted wire were stuck in my fingers. I was given a beating for leaving the class without permission and another for wetting myself in class. In front of the rest of the class, they made me get tissues and clean up the mess. I didn't see my father again. But the memory haunted me for the next six years. In the end, I had to find him. I heard, slowly, that he'd got a job and was working in London."

"When you're 13, what do you really know of a city? I thought I could go there and just find him. It would be that easy. It was early in the year and bitterly cold. I suppose seeing another soulless Christmas and New Year had got me thinking of Dad. After two weeks in London, trying to avoid the authorities who would have taken me back to the home in Liverpool, I was cold and hungry. When I first saw him, he had a smile that would've warmed anybody. He called himself the Reverend Peter. He took me back to his house and looked after me, fed me, got me clothes. Nice clothes, I remember that."

And he helped me. There were a few others there, like me. Girls and boys. All teenagers. Has it ever dawned on you how many children there are on the streets of London? And people think Thailand's a third-world country. Listen to me, Steven. When you compare Britain and Thailand from my level on the ladder, from Lek's level on the ladder, there's no difference. No fucking difference at all."

"For a month I was happy. Actually happy for once in 13 years of my sad little life. I was warm, I had food, I had clothes. I even had friends."

Charli stopped speaking. She stared across the hole at the trees on the other side of the river. She listened to the strangled cry of a lone forest bird. Hunt, surprised at her sudden silence after the rhythmic retelling, looked up at her and wondered if she had noticed a movement. He prayed that someone had come through the forest. He looked at her face for something, a sign of panic or of worry. She continued to stare straight ahead at the forest. Her eyes focused in the distance. Hunt was gathering his last remaining energy and was just about to call out for help.

But just as suddenly as she had stopped speaking, she glanced down at him. Her eyes piercing into his. He had to turn his face away from the ice-green stare.

"And then? One morning I woke. I'm not sure where. It wasn't the same house I'd been living in for those few weeks of happiness and security. Try as I might, I don't know. Maybe I'd been drugged, I don't know. But one day I woke, and I was shackled to a metal bed. No mattress. Just the bare springs. And all those nice clothes that'd been given to me were gone."

"Thirteen-years-old, Steven. And shackled naked to a bed. My arms and legs were bruised and bleeding. And I had difficulty breathing from the beating I'd been given. I was trembling uncontrollably from fear as I struggled against the shackles. But any struggle was futile. I just lay there and wet myself. Just like I did in class."

"There're still times, too many times, when I wake up in the night seeing that room and remembering. Memory's a strange thing. There're many times when events disappear into the depths of my mind. So many other things have happened since. And then, for no particular reason, they surface. Do you find that? They just pop up for no apparent reason."

"For a month at least, maybe more, I stayed chained in that foul, disgusting room. And I got to know the walls very well. The peeling, mouldy wallpaper - pink flowers and vines. The bare floorboards with bits of worn and tattered lino. There was a strange pattern of cubes. Even now when I see one of those optical illusions where you're not sure if you're looking at the outside of a cube or the inside of a box, I break into a cold sweat."

"The cobwebs. My friend the spider. After living in that room, I've never feared spiders. It became the one welcomed visitor each day. The grimy window with the sooty grey lace curtains. Outside the window, I could hear traffic going by. It must have been a quiet street. I lay in that room lonely at night listening to the sounds of a city outside. I watched the shadows change on the walls as the sun went down and it went dark. At 13, shackled to a bed, you see many demons in the gathering night. No need for me to see any horror movies to conjure up those ghosts of childhood. Every night I died. And every morning my hell started again as the light gathered in the window."

"I screamed out for help and was beaten unconscious for doing so. When I came round again, I repeated the process, screaming for help, and was beaten again. It's no fun being beaten, Steven. It hurts physically. But the mental hurt affects you more. When you realise why you're being beaten, you adjust. You adopt a behaviour that reduces the chances of getting beaten. You stop screaming. You look for rewards, little rewards, anything good. That's what breaking in's all about. Learning what to do to get those little rewards. You learn to be grateful."

"Each day, he'd come with food and water. The Reverend Peter. He'd place it by the bed and unlock one arm. I can't eat baked beans or tinned tomatoes on toast, tinned Irish stew, Spam and many other foods. Alphabetti Spaghetti? Every growing kid's favourite? They bring back memories of that faraway room."

"He'd say nothing, and then he'd leave. I'd eat. He'd return and take the plate away. He'd lock my arm back to the bed. Always the same chipped plate and spoon. The same plate. I wanted to throw it away and break it. In an earlier life, I'd have done just that. I'm that kind of person. But he taught me obedience far better than Miss Turnpike or any of the other sadists who had tried, and failed, to educate me, to tame me. I never threw that plate because I knew what would've happened to me if I'd done so. That was my plate and my spoon."

"My toilet was a sand tray under the bed filled with kitty litter. I slept a lot. I think he, or they, drugged the food. But I don't know with what. Maybe you can tell me. You're the expert."

"After the first few weeks, when my bruises had healed, I had visitors. Two, three, sometimes more, a day. Sometimes they'd be with me on their own. Other times the Reverend Peter would sit in. Discussions took place as if I wasn't there. There were foreigners as well. Arabs and Japanese mainly. It didn't take me long to realise I was a commodity about to be sold."

"Over that month, my life changed, Steven. And for 10 years now, it's not been the same. Over that month, I was conditioned. You'd be surprised how easy that happens. When you fear your life's going to be taken away from you, you'll agree to anything. Anything to stay alive. Anything to please."

"It's a bit like training a young puppy. Or a horse. I once told you how I could never keep a pet. I'd do anything, any trick, to make my life a little more comfortable. And believe me, Steven. After a month or more, I was doing anything and everything for them. Thirteen-years-old Steven, and I did everything. Absolutely everything that I was told to do. Because, finally I was a good girl."

"The asking was always with a smile by the dear Reverend Peter and his visitors. It's like breaking a horse. You once asked me if I went horse riding and I gave you my answer quite abruptly. Now you know. I've feelings for the spirits of horses which have been broken. Much like me."

"Ten years later, Steven? Two thousand, probably more, men? I want it all to stop. Can you understand that, Steven?"

He looked up at her. In a weakening voice, he spoke.

"You say you've had 2000 men. I don't know if that's true. What happened to you is paedophilia in my book, Charli. I've never been with a woman younger than 19. Lek, remember her? So again, Charli. Why me? Why this? I didn't do this to you. I'm not the Reverend Fucking Peter. I can guarantee, if I came across him knowing what he'd done, I'd probably kill him for you. So why me?"

Charli snorted at him as she lit another cigarette.

"Why you? Okay, I'll grant you're not the Reverend Peter. But you're the same. You abuse humans. Because, Steven, I've seen the effects of your business at first hand. My world came undone when I was 13. And yet, less than two years later, I'd accepted everything. Can you believe that? At 15, I'd accepted my life and come to terms with it. Looking back at that acceptance, I now know how naive and young and stupid I was. Life? Future? What fucking future? For me I was an animal living day by day with no future to consider."

"Just before my 16th birthday, I woke up. Two weeks before then, I'd had my first needle. And Christ, that was a comforting release. Fucking hell, it was so beautiful. It was almost religious. It beat alcohol any day. And you know how much I like alcohol."

"For 18 months, they put me to work in one of those special places where men who like young kids can go. But by 15 and a half I was getting too old for the sorts of men that like that kind of thing. Anyhow, my owner had got his money back on his investment. So now he put me to work on the streets. He put me with Kim. I'd known Kim for a year. We had a room together. She was my best, my closest, friend. Two years older than me, she knew everything. And she took care of me. The big sister I'd always dreamed of. Usually we'd sleep together. Hold each other closely. I loved Kim. And Kim loved me."

"And then? I came back one day and she was dead. She was just 18 and had seen and had known and had done everything. She'd looked after me for over a year. I learned a lot from her. And then she was dead."

"That was the biggest lesson Kim ever taught me, Steven. The biggest fucking lesson. And just in time. Have you ever seen anyone dead, Steven? Your mother? Father? Brother? Sister? A stranger in a road accident? Have you? I mean really dead. Up close so you can smell it all. Not a photograph. Not a video. Death has a smell, you know."

"Sixteen fucking years old I was, Steven. I'd never seen a dead person before. Never smelt a dead person before. And I was looking at Kim. I spent almost four hours crying and screaming. I was hysterical. I tried to wake her up. That's how stupid I was. But she just carried on lying there. Dead. Dirt under her fingernails, cracked nail polish. Old worn make-up on her face. Just like me. I didn't have to look in any fucking mirror. I could look at Kim and see me. See me a few years down the line. Knowing I'd look just like her, smell just like her. Dead just like her."

"There was, however, one difference. She had little bruises on her arms. On her legs. Two weeks earlier, Steven, I'd tried the same stuff. Your fucking stuff. I'd tried it for the first time. And it felt good. It felt fucking great. Two weeks earlier, Steven, I'd started something that gave me a release from the waking nightmare. The hell I confronted every day."

"Seeing Kim like she was in the bathroom, seeing what she'd become and what I was becoming, I thought briefly of killing myself then. Shooting up a massive load and going to join Kim wherever she'd gone. I really did."

"Four fucking hours I screamed my heart out, Steven. For Kim. For what had happened to her. And for me. Selfishly, importantly, for me. For what had happened to me. For what was happening. I was scared, Steven. Really, truly fucking shit-scared. For the first time in my small, minuscule, insignificant fucking life, I thought about the future and what it held for me. And, when I looked, there was no hope. There was no future. There was nothing."

Charli again paused in her retelling of the past. The forest was quiet, and Hunt again hoped that she had heard somebody coming through the forest. This was his only slim chance now of being saved.

"And then? I stopped crying. And I've not cried since. I'm 23-years-old, Steven. In almost seven years, Steven, I've not shed a single tear. Why should I?"

"I ran the bath for Kim. I still remember making sure the water wasn't too hot for her. Kim always hated the water too hot. I undressed her body. It's not easy when somebody's dead. I even pleaded with her to help me. I put her, as gently as I could, in the bath and I cleaned her. All the while, I made sure her head stayed above the water. I hated it when the water went up my nose. And I know - knew - she did also. Don't ask me why I did these things for her. To this day, I don't know why I did all of this. I was just 16. I dragged her body out of the bath. I said sorry to her when her thigh thumped on the floor."

"I dried her. I dressed her in clean clothes. Her best clothes. There was a jacket of mine she always wanted to borrow. We had a fight once, our only fight, when she wore the jacket without asking me. It was the only time I fought with Kim. I put the jacket on her. I finally gave it to her. I removed all the cracked nail varnish. I thought of re-applying some new varnish but decided not to. I placed her gently on my bed. Kim had two favourite teddy bears. I placed one in her arms. I took the other."

"Look at those pictures, Steven. Think about me. Look at those emerald, fucking sea-green eyes and think about what was going through my mind just months after she'd died. Think about your business, Steven. Think about how much stuff you've transported. If you deal with South America, I'm certain, now, it's not just cut flowers. How many lives, like Kim's, like mine and like Lek's, have you touched Steven? How many lives have you poisoned? How many flowers have you cut? Have you killed? Think about that."

Charli got up and walked back to the shade. She lit another cigarette and returned to the hole. She continued.

"As I left Kim, I made a promise. To her, or to myself, I'm not sure. There were no more tears in my eyes, Steven, but I promised her I'd make things right for me and, one day, for her. It wasn't easy. The shit who herded Kim and me and others was after me. Looking out, no doubt, for his investment. He'd not made a full return yet on my cunt and all he had to show was a dead body which had to be disposed of. That costs money. While the police might have no hope of finding missing children in London, the underworld's got every possible means."

"I had other friends who could help and did. I made a plan. Partly by my own ingenuity, partly by good luck, one way or another it's generally worked. I've no idea how it worked. Because I spent much of the next two years in an alcoholic haze, sometimes on drugs, your drugs maybe, flat on my back having sex with anybody and any way just to make money. Money, money, money. But I saved. I conditioned myself to do things my way. After seeing Kim and the needle marks, I swore off the needles. It wasn't easy. On my eighteenth birthday, I even quit smoking. Only the occasional one since then."

Charli lit another cigarette.

"I tried to give up drinking but failed. You can't be good at everything, I suppose. Alcohol's my one vice, my one relaxation from this still far too cruel world. Given the amount I drink, it'll probably kill me long before any HIV may kick in."

"Those pictures, Steven, believe it or not, represent promotion. Slowly, I moved out of the mass-fuck sex-on-the-streets industry. I slept with fewer slobs but made, perversely, more money. It's amazing what some sick fucks will pay to watch you pee in your knickers. I eventually developed a very select clientele of 10 or 12 regulars. City types. Some of London's finest captains of industry. I had to be just the right age for them, 16 to 18. Any younger and it was too much of a risk for them. As I said, the real paedos were interested in me only 'til I reached 15."

"Even now, I'm quite proud of what I did for myself from 17 to 20. I'm sure, looking back, that I didn't fool any of them. They all knew what I was. But I tried reading a bit and learning a bit. Now I'm a very avid reader. If I overheard one of them mention a book, I'd rush out and buy it. And read it. And I'd take delight in discussing it the next time I saw them. Back then, to them, I must've looked foolish. I half-hoped one of the captains of industry might establish me as a mistress. Looking back, that was also a stupid idea. What chance, really, has an uneducated, however bright, 17-year-old got of being a serious partner to some high-flying businessman? I was just a bit of dessert on the side. I was a dispensable toy. To be used and thrown aside when I got too expensive. But they used me and I used them. It worked well. And I saved. Money, money, money, Steven. Save, save, save."

"I'd even started to make plans for retirement. Careful investments with good advice from some of the captains helped. When you reach that level in the prostitution business, it isn't necessary to cost things out by the fuck or suck. It's understood that your needs are looked after. And I was well looked after. Help with a flat here, some clothes there. A car here, investments there. I'd turned my life around. And although I say so myself, I'm quite proud of what I achieved."

"And then? And then along came Sir Gordon Fucking Wessel. Remember him, Steven? In one night, he almost pushed me right back to where I thought I'd crawled so far from. I'd always hated his kinky games. They repulsed me. But he looked after me well and I always gave in to his disgusting perversions. I'd seen a lot over the years, but he was dangerously perverted. As I discovered to my cost."

"After the last night I spent with him, I awoke right back where I'd started. Beaten, bruised, and bound to my own fucking bed. The batteries of the two vibrators he'd left inside me had long since died. Blood, my blood, was crusted all over the bed. My right shoulder was dislocated. And I'm sure that was the only thing that saved me. Being dislocated, I could slowly release my left arm by twisting on my dislocated right. The sensation was sickening. I threw up and almost choked to death. When I eventually freed myself, I learned I'd been unconscious for more than a day. He must've left me for dead. Of that, I'm sure. He must've been crazy. Panicked and crazy."

"Apart from Kim, I'd one more friend and confidant. Malcolm, a photographer who took many of the pictures you've seen. He was a lovely man. The closest male friend I've ever had. Apart, maybe, from John. When I set up my private pad for the big boys, Mal gave me the best advice and help. Hidden cameras. With most clients, I'd stopped using them. But not with Sir Kinky Gordo Weirdo Wessel. In some ways at least, when you deal with the quick fuck end of the spectrum, you know what it's all about. But public-school captains of industry? They're weird. I mean, they're really fucking kinky. And none more so than Wessel."

"You asked me how I could do all of this to you, Steven? It's easy. I've had experience. I've brought down bigger fucking game than you. I may not have pulled the trigger on Wessel, but I know the real reason he killed himself. It took me two weeks to get myself sorted out after his visit. I was a recluse. I was trying, for a few days at least, to drink myself to death. Always my cop-out. Whenever I've wanted to kill myself, I've been too scared to slash my wrists or jump off some tall building. Instead, I just drink and drink and I hope I won't wake up one morning. But always I have."

"And so, I woke one morning with no more alcohol in the flat. Since first regaining consciousness, I hadn't left the flat. I'd eaten all the food and gone through all of my well-stocked drinks cabinet. My head was thumping with the alcohol and my right arm was still dislocated. There was a doctor I'd known in the past. From my days on the streets. For a price, he looked after all the girls. He helped with treating sexual diseases and all the other problems that a teenage hooker couldn't get treated on the national health. At least not without a shit-load of awkward questions being asked and social workers appearing on white horses over the nearest hill. What he did was illegal and, therefore, expensive. But he was good, he was efficient, and he was clean."

"I cleaned myself up as much as possible and went to see him. He relocated my arm, fixed me up, and sent me on my way again. Just like in the past. The bad old days. His final words to me were: I thought I'd seen the last of you a few years back, Charli. You're a bright girl and don't belong here. Get a grip and move on."

"As I left his surgery, I passed the Thai Embassy and idly saw a poster about 'Visit Thailand Year'. Around the corner, sitting in a pub, my arm strapped across my breast, trying to eat sausage and chips with one hand, I made my plan. I got a grip and decided to finally move on. I now had a burning hatred, a desire for revenge, for Wessel, and I was going to go out of my way to get him. I decided to develop the pictures, dump them on him and his wife, and then go for a holiday until the heat died down. I chose Thailand by chance because I'd seen the advertisement."

"Dumping those photographs on his desk gave me such a high. Far better than any of your fucking heroin, Steven. I caused such an uproar when I got into his office. He was so powerful he managed to get the whole thing suppressed from the papers. I'd hoped he'd fail, finally. He could buy off his staff better than any tabloid. And he did. There were rumours, of course. But the tabloids never got near the truth. The best they came up with was suggesting a link with his secretary. For a bit of inside info, Steven, I can tell you he was fucking her as well. Lady Liz knew this. She's a very clever lady. No matter how much he kept secret from her, he was no match for her intelligence. I suspect if it'd just continued with his secretary, the occasional lover, or even the occasional high class call girl, she might've let it go at that. But not me. She couldn't let this one go."

"The ecstasy of dropping the pictures on his desk was only surpassed by giving a similar, fat envelope to his wife. I drove straight to her house after seeing him. Seeing those pictures of what he did to me, she was going to divorce him just when the big deal, his big deal, was going through. I met Lady E twice. Once when I gave her the pictures and once in a wine bar. My God, Steven, she's a powerful woman. Frighteningly so."

"I can see why Wessel's still successful. She's twice the man he never really was. Makes Margaret Thatcher look like a little kitten. In both meetings with me, it was clear that she utterly despised me. She accused me and my 'kind' of being wreckers of families. You and I know that's not true, Steven. But I was in no mood to argue or philosophise. She had a deal for me. She wanted everything kept out of the papers. For my silence, I was guaranteed 10,000 shares in the company at prices before the takeover. And you know what happened to them, Steven. Not bad, considering the thought of exposing Gordie had never crossed my mind. I'd only wanted to throw a spanner into the family works. She kept her promise, I'll give her that. You know? In a way, I admire her. How she ever got landed with him, I'll never know. As a sort of reward, my shares in Wessel are now worth more than 500,000 pounds. Crazy, don't you think?"

"And then he killed himself. Bang, just like that. He couldn't bear to lose. When Lady E told me of the shares, she also told me of the planned takeover. And she told me she was going to tell Wessel that evening before the takeover that she'd start divorce proceedings immediately after the papers were signed. She told me she'd name his secretary, Sarah Wilmington, as co-respondent in the divorce papers. All I can assume is, she kept to her word and that, I reckon, was why he shot himself. It was no fucking accident, Steven. Whatever the papers say. He'd lost and he knew it. I'd won. And Lady E was the executioner."

"The funny thing was that she, Lady E, had already been in touch with me. She wanted the true extent of the scandal hidden. Only his secretary was going to be implicated. And Lady E took care of that in her own inimitable style. In the end, Wessel did everyone a favour. For my silence, I got shares from Lady E in Wessel Enterprises. Wessel had very nearly killed me. But thanks, perversely, to him, I'm now comfortably off. I already had a tidy little nest-egg put aside. But with the WE shares, I'm secure. Since then my life changed, finally, for the better. No man's been near me in all that time. He, Wessel, was the last person to ever fuck me. That, Steven, is why you had no hope."

"This life's nearly over for me. Did you guess that? I've almost made everything right. For Kim, for Lek, and importantly for me. Do you feel privileged? You're the first person I've told this to. Not Lek. Not John, nor Jay. Not anybody. I've got to go now. I need to get back to Bangkok. I won't be seeing you again."

Chapter 22

These last words hit Hunt harder than the bullets. He screamed out.

"What about me, Charli? How do I get out? You can't leave me here. Surely?"

"I can, Steven. Surely. I'm tying up all the loose ends in my life. You, most definitely, are a very loose end. Got that? Who's going to find you?"

"This trail. You told me it's a popular trail. What happens when some walkers come across the river and find me?"

Charli burst into a fit of laughter.

"Oh Steven, that's so precious. You're wonderful. Have you noticed many people over the last few days? I haven't."

"The weekend, Charli. It's a public holiday. There'll be hordes of people here. You said it yourself about the bird-watching group. They're bound to find me. Somebody'll hear me. And then what?"

"Sorry Steven. There's no chance of you being found. Ever. Remember how many people looked for Jim Thompson? You told me his story yourself. And they knew where to bloody well look, for God's sake. Who will know where to look for you, Steven? Who? Who the fuck knows you're here? Your maid? This is one small river flowing from Khao Yai. You're a million fucking miles from humanity."

For the first time in days, Hunt got a clear look at Charli. The sun was beginning its fall and her face was illuminated. She stood over his hole and he looked up at her feet balanced on the edge. Up along the length of the velveteen skirt and the shadow of the underneath of her breasts. He saw her chin pointed to the sky as she raised her arms wide. He saw her suck in her breath and then shout out loud.

"Hello everybody. Steven Hunt is stuck in a hole and in need of some attention. I shot him. My name is Charli Harris. Come and help him."

She drew out the last word. The forest was startled. Cicadas stopped calling and the birds went silent. A breeze ruffled the leaves of trees that lined the river valley. In the distance, there was the low but perceptible rumble of thunder. Charli looked down at Hunt. She shrugged her shoulders.

"Sorry Steven. Nobody here. Want me to give it another go just in case?"

"There's every chance. Fucking hell, Charli. This is a trail. Used by people."

Her laughter hit him hard.

"Oh, dear me, Steven. I love it. You're wonderful. Do you really think I'd be stupid enough to spend three, four days with you, like this, on a popular trail? Come on Steven. Credit me with something. I may only be a mere woman. I may, even, only be a mere prostitute."

She screamed the next words at him.

"But I'm not fucking stupid. So, for fuck's sake, credit me with a bit of intelligence. In the immortal words of George Bush; Read my lips. Steven, you will not be found. I promise you that."

Charli calmed herself down. Her hands were shaking and her neck muscles went tight. She took another cigarette out and lit it. She blew the first roll of smoke down to him. She continued talking to him in a measured voice.

"Where I parked the car the first day with you? And where I've parked that car every day since? There - is - a – trail, Steven. It's nine kilometres from the headquarters. It's a trail, but it's not popular. Nine fucking kilometres. This? This, Steven, isn't a trail. Except maybe for wild animals and the occasional poacher. I found some old discarded batteries a few days back."

"I doubt very much whether another human being's ever come down to this river here. Did you notice any discarded water bottles, cigarette packets? The usual signs of humanity you find along even the remotest forest trails? Did you? Sorry, Steven, now I have to go."

"It's rained the last three days, I think. The rainy season's come a little earlier than I'd expected. Let's blame it on El Niño. Everyone else does now. This river is really quite impressive when it's in full flow. For the next six months, Steven, the river bed, and by that I also mean your little residence here, will be under water. A lot of water. Billions of fucking gallons of the stuff. Give or take a pint or two."

"And, your home, this hole? Have you considered how it got formed? I've tried to wonder how many thousands of years it's taken those stones at the bottom there to grind out this hole. Like some giant pestle and mortar. Every rainy season, they get to churn their way round the inside of that hole. Grind, grind, grind, Steven. Churn, churn, churn. After six months of churning and grinding about with you at the bottom, there won't be very much left to find of you or your fancy clothes. I think I've thought of everything. Don't you?"

Charli gave Hunt an impish smile. She turned and walked back to her bag. He screamed after her. She packed the bag and cleared up the litter. She stared a while at the black stain where his blood had first been spilt on the rocks. The smoothed rocks caught the sunlight. For anyone wanting a beautiful spot to sunbathe by the river and its waterfall, this was ideal.

She listened to him screaming. Even though she was only 10 metres from him, his voice sounded feeble. There was one small bottle of whisky left. Charli picked it up. As she walked to the hole for the last time, she unravelled a length of rope. She dropped the bottle into his lap.

"This is for you. And this rope, Steven? It offers you the only way out you can have. I'm not entirely callous. Goodbye."

Chapter 23

Charli began her walk through the forest and back to the car for the final time. There was a light-headed feeling that had little to do with the alcohol. As the sun was going down, occasional shafts of light broke through the increasing gloom of the late-afternoon forest. She reached a small clearing where a tree had fallen, opening up the forest to the sky. As she looked up, she could see the clouds racing to fill the blue spaces in the sky. A cloud moved across the sun and darkness fell over the forest. The birds went quiet. The cicadas stopped their otherwise incessant trilling.

Over the last few days, Charli had been aware of thunder in the distant hills of the mountain range. As she moved off once more through the forest, the thunder rolled louder than before. Charli increased her pace as a strong wind rattled the upper canopy of the forest. The birds were still silent but the cicadas had resumed their chorus. As Charli reached the road, there was a tremendous crash as thunder blasted the trees nearby. But there was no lightning.

Leaden with six months of waiting, the sky had turned black and the raindrops now fell. Large and heavy. Charli walked along the road, back to her car. The sky seemed to sense her because, as quickly as the rain had started, it suddenly stopped. Charli took her time now and gazed at the forest around her. She watched as the upper branches of the trees swayed and seemingly waved goodbye to her in the increasing wind. Wind that Charli knew from experience preceded a tropical storm. The first of many for this monsoon season. She listened to the sound of tree branches thrashing against each other.

Charli reached the bridge where the river passed under the road. She had always been in a hurry to get across the bridge and back to the car, fearful of being seen on a deserted stretch of road. But not now. She leaned on the edge of the bridge and gazed at the river. The wind blew about Charli and leaves rushed past her in a hurry to go someplace. There was a gentle stream of water rolling languidly between the boulders. It was making a gurgling sound that hadn't been apparent just a few days before when she had first stopped here.

Charli heard the noise in the distance but made no move to seek cover. Four motor bikes came past her belching their trademark blue smoke. She could hear the long-haired teenage boys shout out 'farang' as they went by. Charli sneered and crossed to the other side of the road to peer over this part of the bridge for the first time. She was looking down into a deep bedrock gorge. She opened the picnic hamper and took out his house keys, his watch, and his wallet. She looked at them. She pocketed the keys. She flung the watch and wallet as far as she could into the gorge. When the pieces landed, she could not see them despite straining hard to see. Finally, she continued walking back to the car.

At the car, Charli slowly placed everything that she had carried from the forest into the boot. She had the same feeling that had often plagued her childhood. A feeling where nothing seemed real. It was as if she was living in a daydream. A strong wind blew again and rattled the surrounding trees, their branches, their leaves. She stared up at the swaying branches of the trees. Thunder again crashed into the forest close by but this time it was preceded by lightning. Charli looked at her grimy clothes. She opened her case and selected another loose-fitting skirt and a T-shirt.

A crash of thunder followed a lightning bolt, which seemed to hit the road nearby. Charli listened to an unfamiliar sound that was moving rapidly through the forest. It sounded like a million leaves were falling as the rainstorm struck. Large, heavy raindrops suddenly bounced from the roof of her car. Charli quickly pulled the skirt off and turned to take the new skirt from the boot.

Charli raised her head up to the sky as it washed her face. She remained in this position for minutes. Thunder and lightning crashed all about her but finally, almost perversely, Charli felt completely relaxed and completely safe. Nobody and nothing could, or would, hurt her now. Finally, Charli removed her T-shirt and placed it on the roof of the car to get wet. She stood and wiped the dirt from her body with the ever-falling rain. She used the sodden T-shirt as a sponge. Once again clean, Charli prepared the clothes. To prevent getting too wet, she dressed quickly, throwing the dirty clothes into the back of the car. Closing everything up, she drove off.

In the forest, the colours were grey, brown, and green. Here on the road it was grey; grey for the sky and grey for the road. Green and brown bordered the grey, nature's living vegetation juxtaposing the man-made drabness of the road. Charli had the windscreen wipers working hard to brush away not just the falling rain drops but also the leaves blowing from the forest.

Some 200 kilometres north, an old man had been caught by the same storm. The gypsum roof that his devoted daughter had toiled so hard to get for him had developed cracks. It had lasted no longer than the thatch roofs he used to make from material he gathered for free from the forest. Water rained in from several points, flooding his modest home. The old man thought of what he must do to get this repaired. He had the money now. Not like last year.

Driving carefully through the forest, Charli watched it come alive, repeating the circle it had made for a million years or more. As quickly as it had started, the rain stopped. Steam now rose from the road. At each bend, a small river of water flowed, taking the line of least resistance. The thunder continued to boil around her and she watched as she drove through the fall of a million leaves. At the park exit, the ranger rushed to open the gate and get back to the sanctuary of his booth. He was a minor intrusion to her reverie.

The forest disappeared in her rear-view mirror as Charli headed onto the rice plains. The sky above was black. But in the distance, on the horizon, there was a whiteness, and for a moment, Charli thought of it as her own personal light at the end of the tunnel. The green fields of newly planted rice, rice planted in anticipation of these coming rains, contrasted with the grey-black sky. Charli drove through this all in a euphoric daze. She saw details she had never noticed before. A small hut stood in the middle of a sea of green. Clustered in this were nine or ten people seeking shelter from the incessant rain. Charli waved at them, but they could not possibly see her.

A frail old woman, bent double with her years, led a massive buffalo along the side of the road, oblivious to the rain. The buffalo had two horns that spanned more than two metres. One was turned up. The other was turned down. Occasionally, the old woman stopped to spit out blood red saliva. The by-product of her betel-chewing habit. The buffalo trotted dutifully behind her. When it stopped to take some grass, the old woman never turned around. If she felt the rope go tight in her hand, she merely gave it a tug. And both continued on their way as they had done for so many thousands of years.

A wooden shack by the side of the road doubled as a shop and meeting place. At one corner was a red earthenware water butt. Empty for many months, but now the rain falling on the roof was being channelled into it. Charli glimpsed three naked children who laughed and played under the shower that filled the water butt. A mangy dog, its tail between its legs, trotted along the side of the road. Three schoolgirls, caught by the sudden storm, ran barefoot along the road, clutching their school bags to their chests. Along the canal, a small boat filled with watermelons crossed to the other side. The surface of the canal was a mass of ripples from the falling rain.

The ritualised Songkran festival marked the start of the Thai new year. Climate change now usually brought the rains in the middle of May, but not this year. This year, the start of the rains would coincide with Songkran. A rarity nowadays. Water that had been preciously conserved over the last six months was now thrown everywhere. As a thousand or more water butts began to fill with the first rains of the new season, young children made their own special Songkran, splashing about in the puddles and throwing cup loads of water at their friends. Meanwhile, the teenagers and adults went about the serious business of preparing the lands for the new rice. A practice that had gone on largely unchanged for 4000 years or more.

As she drove, Charli saw two girls, maybe 17, their sodden clothes clinging to their slender bodies as they jogged barefoot along the roadside. They carried bamboo poles over each shoulder. Each pole was laden with young rice seedlings that had been planted in nurseries. These were being borne to the vast oceans of brown mud that stretched into the distance and which would soon be a field of green.

Caught out by the early rains, the village elders had to determine which fields should be planted first. Charli could see the elderly men ploughing the brown mud that had been parched by months of sun. Few farmers relied any more on water buffaloes. For ploughing, they now used the all-purpose E-tarn – an engine on wheels with an overly long steering handle. Charli passed one that was towing a trailer filled with laughing, smiling villagers. Everyone was soaked by the deluge, but it didn't matter. The whole life of the community depended on these rains and after six dry months, the new season was beginning again.

Approaching Bangkok, the environment changed subtly. Villages appeared untidier. Fields lay abandoned. On some were billboards that advertised land for sale for housing projects. Still closer to the city, it was possible to see construction sites that had once been fields. In an abandoned village next to one such project was an old man who would not change and who would not move. Last year had been the last year of his village. He stood in the driving rain and gazed at the construction site about him. For the first time in his life, he had some money but no work to do. It felt strange. His tears were masked by the driving rain. He wanted to plant his rice. But he had no field.

As Charli approached the outskirts of Bangkok, she slowed the car as traffic density increased. With this final approach, the first storm of the season abated. The gleaming concrete, steel, and glass shone in the shafts of sunlight that pierced the grey-black clouds. For the old man in his abandoned village, life would never be the same. For this, Charli was sorry. She did not know him and could do nothing for him. For Lek's father, life could never be the same. For this, Charli knew she could and she would help. And for herself, Charli knew that her lifecycle had been broken. And for the first time that she could ever recall, she felt there might just possibly be a future. Charli knew that her future was uncertain. But now, for the first time, she had a future.

Chapter 24

Charli checked her baggage in and drifted through passport control. She sat for a long time in the restaurant, watching planes landing and taking off. As she watched, she drank some wine and smoked a cigarette. When it was time to board, she drifted through the X-ray check and into the final departure lounge. She tried to read from her magazine but could not. The period before getting on the plane had always been the least enjoyable to her.

Charli had reserved a seat by the window as always. A couple sat next to her and smiled but said nothing. She continued to stare out of the window and into the night. As the 747 taxied to the end of the rain-soaked runway, Charli looked out toward the terminal buildings. She caught her reflection in the window. The plane arced right as it lined itself at the end of the runway.

There was a gathering roar as the 747 accelerated down the runway. Charli stared straight ahead of her. The man sitting next to her looked at her. The nose of the plane lifted from the ground and they were airborne. As they climbed, the plane turned and Charli was looking straight down through the window at the lights of the city below. She raised her arm slightly and waved.

"Bye bye."

She gritted her teeth and looked forward. The passenger next to her had watched this.

"Oh, don't be like that, pet. There's always next year. Me'n Sylvia here'd never been to Thailand before. When Sylv suggested goin', ah thought she meant Tahiti. Ah said to her, didn't ah Sylv, that's where they wear all them grass skirts and no bra? Had ta look at a map, just ta find tha place. But we 'ad a great time in Patt-aye-are. We're definitely savin' up ta come again next year. Pattaya beats Redcar beach any day. Heaven on Earth ah call it. Don't ah, Sylv?"

There was a single note as the lights came on saying that seat belts could be removed. Charli excused herself and went to the toilet. She felt sick and vomited into the bowl.

As Thailand was left behind, time dragged. It felt like the longest flight that Charli had endured. Trevor and Sylvia tried to engage her in conversation with their stories of Pattaya - Heaven on Earth. When they asked Charli if she had been to Pattaya, she said no. A little tersely.

"There ya go then. Get savin' fer next year and go ta Pattaya. You'll have a great time. I even got Sylv into a girlie bar. She loved it. Looking at all them little girlies in their sexy G-strings. Didn't ya Pet?"

Sylvia did not answer.

More than 11 hours later, the plane began its approach to London Heathrow. Charli had been staring out of the window for some time watching the lights of Europe go by beneath. Former baby care hostess Rattana had been given her first command as Chief Air Hostess – the youngest at Thai International. As the 747 began its approach to Heathrow, she came on the intercom. She took out the paper that she had written her first landing speech on.

"Ladies and gentlemen. Thai International flight TG911 is about to land at London Heathrow Airport. The weather on the ground is clear with an unseasonal ground frost. The temperature is -1 Centigrade. For that, I'm sorry."

"On behalf of Captain Taksin and the rest of the crew, I'd like to thank you all for flying Thai. We hope those of you who visited Thailand will please come back again and we hope that those of you who transited will stay longer next time. On behalf of the crew, I'd like to wish every one of you a pleasant journey wherever you may be going."

"As we begin the approach, could you please raise your seats and tables to the upright positions. Thank you."

Charli drifted through passport control and collected her bags. She could see the Darlington couple that had sat next to her on the plane on the other side of the conveyor belt. She tried to avoid catching their attention. She wheeled her trolley through the green channel, watching as the customs routinely stopped people. She realised now that they knew what to look for. And she wondered if another Lek had been on this flight. But she knew also that they were getting grams or kilograms when tonnes were passing through elsewhere. She felt the weight of the floppy disks in her pocket and wondered what she would do with this.

Charli wandered through the sea of people. There was a long queue for taxis. Freezing passengers from Thailand and other equally exotic destinations waited patiently as taxis pulled up. Charli joined the back of the queue and rolled her eyes when she saw Trevor and Sylvia join the same queue less than three behind her.

"Wow. Fancy meetin' you 'ere."

Charli smiled wanly and continued to look ahead at the interminably long line. At first, she did not register the sound of the car horn. But as people looked beyond the taxis, Charli looked as well.

The Rolls Royce was parked on its own. The back door was open, and a figure was moving across the road toward her.

"Oh, thank God, Charli. Bloody London traffic, it's worse than Bangkok. Yai and Jay telephoned to me with your flight details and suggested I should collect you from the airport."

He picked up her cases and walked them back toward the Rolls. Charli smiled weakly at Trevor and Sylvia. She had not expected this and was taken aback. But not as much as they were.

"Well, bugger me."

That was all Trevor could utter as the Rolls pulled silently away.

Trevor and Sylvia were left staring at the sad face of the passenger they never got to know during the 11 hours of the flight. Sitting in the back of the Rolls Royce, Charli looked out of the window at nothing. Her purple business suit, piped with black, looked as if it belonged in the Rolls. Trevor looked once again as a fleeting image had formed and disappeared just as quickly from his mind before he could capture it. If he had been able to see properly, he would have made out the image of a white tiger and a confident young Thai woman who were now Charli's life-guardians.

Sir John reached towards the drink cabinet.

"You must be freezing, lassie. Laphroaig, that'll warm you up. Doctor's orders. I'm having one and all I did was carry your bags."

Charli obeyed and took the drink. She looked at Sir John and smiled. A thin smile.

"I got your message, Charli. But I must say that it came as a surprise. I wanted to phone you but you were pretty explicit about that. So, I didn't. Yai told me you were coming on this flight and he said that I should meet you. And I have. Just. Is everything all right? No problems?"

"Everything's okay, John. There're no problems. It's all finished now. After 10 years, it's all finally over."

Sir John Cormack knew better than to question her further. He knew that when the time was right, she would tell him everything. But until then, he could wait. Sir John watched Charli as she stared straight ahead, trying to control herself. He was sure she was about to cry, but she did not. She held out the empty glass. He filled it. She drank it.

"You've a beautiful daughter, John. Jay's a credit to you. She's got a good heart. Jai dee. It's not important what other people think,

John. Not important. Take it from me. You should see more of your daughter, John. And you should see more of her mother."

THE END

Charli will return. Eighteen months on, she has a sense of humour, she is still out for more revenge, but she now has the freedom that money gives to help her. She also has an unlikely ally; Lady Elizabeth Wessel.

Charli returns in 2023 in

Justice of the White Tiger